From the corner of her eye, Katie saw a boy with red hair who was about her age. He stood near the doorway, looking nervous. With a start, she realized he was watching her, because he kept diverting his gaze when she glanced his way. *Odd*, Katie told herself. Katie had a nagging sense she'd seen him before, even though she couldn't place him. As nonchalantly as possible, she rolled her wheelchair closer, picking up a magazine as she passed a table.

She flipped through the magazine, pretending to be interested, all the while glancing discreetly toward the boy. Even though he also picked up a magazine, Katie could tell that he was preoccupied with studying her. Suddenly, she grew self-conscious. Was something wrong with the way she looked? She'd thought she looked better than she had in months when she'd left her hospital room that afternoon. Why was he watching her?

ALSO AVAILABLE IN DELL LAUREL-LEAF BOOKS

ONE LAST WISH

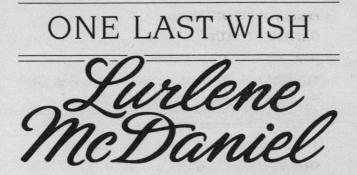

Someone Dies,
Someone Lives

Published by
Dell Laurel-Leaf
an imprint of
Random House Children's Books
a division of Random House, Inc.
New York

Visit us on the Web! www.randomhouse.com/teens

**Educators and librarians, for a variety of teaching tools, visit us at
www.randomhouse.com/teachers**

Visit Lurlene McDaniel's Web site! www.lurlenemcdaniel.com

ISBN: 0-553-29842-9

RL: 5.0

Reprinted by arrangement with Bantam Books

Printed in the United States of America

First Dell Laurel-Leaf Edition March 2003

20 19 18

OPM

Someone Dies, Someone Lives

One

Dear Katie,

You don't know me, but I know about you, and because I do, I want to give you a special gift. Accompanying this letter is a certified check, my gift to you, with no strings attached, to spend on anything you want. No one knows about this gift except you, and you are free to tell anyone you want.

Who I am isn't really important, only that you and I have much in common. Through no fault of our own, we have endured pain and isolation and have spent many days in a hospital feeling lonely and scared. I hoped for a miracle, but most of all I hoped for someone to truly understand what I was going through.

*I can't make you live longer, I can't stop you from
hurting. But I can give you one wish, as someone
did for me. My wish helped me find purpose, faith,
and courage.*

*Friendship reaches beyond time, and the true mir-
acle is in giving, not receiving. Use my gift to fulfill your wish.*

> *Your Forever Friend,*
> *JWC*

KATIE O'ROARK REREAD the letter that had mysteriously appeared in the drawer of her bedside table
at the hospital two weeks before. It had been in a
long envelope, sealed with red wax and stamped
with *OLW*, for the One Last Wish Foundation. She
remembered the numbing shock she'd experienced
as she read the letter and found a certified check
for one hundred thousand dollars. No matter how
many times she went over the letter, she was unable to figure out the identity of her benefactor.
The check, made out to her and signed by a Richard Holloway, whom she'd also never heard of, was
hers to spend on anything she wanted. Her parents
couldn't figure it out, either, but it was no joke. The
money was now in the bank.

"Still trying to solve that mystery?" her mother
asked, coming into Katie's bedroom. "Your father's
tried everything he knows and can't come up with
an answer."

Katie's dad was a reporter on an Ann Arbor
newspaper, and had access to computer banks of

data and information. If anyone could find out about the Foundation, Dan O'Roark could. Even he couldn't, though.

"It bothers me, not knowing who'd give me so much money," Katie said. "I want to know who and why."

"Don't think about it. If the generous JWC wanted you to know, he or she wouldn't act so secretive. Let's just be grateful."

Katie adjusted the flexible tubing attached to the oxygen tank beside her bed and leaned wearily against her pillow. The money was a fantastic gift all right, but how could it buy her the one thing she needed most? No amount of money could purchase her a new heart.

"I came up to tell you that Melody's here. She wants to see you. Are you up to visitors?" her mother asked.

Melody Bernelli, Katie's sixteen-year-old best friend, stopped by every day after school. Katie wanted to see her, but couldn't deny that Melody's visits were becoming harder emotionally. Melody reminded her too much of the "normal" world she'd had to leave behind months before. "Sure, Mom. Tell her to come up," Katie replied, tucking the letter under her sheet.

Minutes later, Melody bounced into the room, her brown eyes wide with concern. "Your mom said you had a bad night." Melody dragged a chair over to the bed. "I won't stay long, but I just had to see you, Katie. I almost skipped last period today because I got this horrible feeling that you were worse and that I wasn't going to get to see you again."

Katie smiled, although the effort cost her. Even the smallest tasks robbed her of strength. "I'm no worse," she assured her friend. "No better, either."

"I just can't believe this is happening to you," Melody wailed. "How will the track team manage without you next spring?"

Ann Arbor High was a big school with well over twelve hundred students in attendance. The girls' junior year had just barely begun. "Coach Hudson stopped by last night," Katie said. "She tried to give me a pep talk, but unless a miracle happens, I won't be running track again."

"Mrs. Collins wants to do an article in the school newspaper about you."

Katie frowned. "I wouldn't like that. Dad's already run one in his sports column about me. I hate having half of Michigan knowing about my problems."

"Why? When he writes about you, he's impartial. He never gives our school's track team more space than any other. Even last year, when we won all-city and you had the best time on your leg of the relay race. This time, it's different, Katie. This time, if more people read about what's happening to you, maybe you'll have a better chance."

"Better chance for what?" Katie asked as she took deep breaths of oxygen. "My only chance is to get a new heart. Who's got one to spare?"

Melody hung her head, and Katie saw that her eyes had filled with tears. "Don't cry, Melly—it won't help, and it makes me feel bad," Katie whispered.

Melody grabbed a tissue from the table next to the bed and dabbed her eyes. "I can't help it. It's all so unfair! Why did this happen to you?"

Katie had no answers. The past few months of her life seemed like a nightmare. She'd gotten a cold—a simple, ordinary cold—last May. It had persisted, and no matter what she did, she couldn't shake the lingering fatigue and shortness of breath. Soon, even climbing the stairs to her room had become a chore. She'd experienced dizzy spells, and although it was June, she'd felt cold all the time.

"You're going to the doctor for a thorough exam," her mother had insisted.

Her family doctor had referred her to the teaching hospital at the University of Michigan, where she'd become the patient of Dr. Curtis, a cardiologist. He put her through various tests. She could hardly complete the treadmill test, a real embarrassment for the girl who'd been named top sophomore sprinter by a vote of all area high school coaches only last spring.

Dr. Curtis told the O'Roarks, "I'm putting Katie in the hospital and getting a complete workup done on her."

"Hospital?" Katie cried. "I don't want to be in the hospital."

"Katie's never been sick a day in her life," her mother declared.

"Well, she's sick now," Dr. Curtis said, "and I want to get to the bottom of it."

Overnight, her world had turned upside down. Katie had been hospitalized, and poked and prodded and tested until she thought she would scream. Dr. Curtis did a heart catheterization, numbing an area in her groin and snaking a thin, flexible tube up an artery into her heart. She watched the procedure on a video monitor as he injected dye through the tube to better see the inside of her heart.

Katie would never forget the day Dr. Curtis had sat her and her parents down in his office and grimly explained, "Katie's suffering from viral cardiomyopathy. Your heart's a muscle. A virus has attacked and destroyed it."

"My heart?" Katie asked, incredulous. At first, her parents were too stunned to react.

Dr. Curtis picked up a plastic model of a heart from his desk and explained the functions of its chambers. "Your heart muscle is weakened and flabby. It's enlarged and having to work twice as hard to deliver oxygen to your blood. That's why you're tired all the time." He reached over and took her hand. "That's why your nail beds and lips look bluish."

He was right. There was a definite bluish cast to her fingertips. She took her hands away and shoved them in her lap.

"What are you going to do about it?" her father asked.

"First, we'll get Katie stabilized, put her on medications, and, I hope, send her home."

Katie's already sick heart was pounding rapidly

and making her feel lightheaded. "Then I can start school in September and resume track?" Katie asked.

The doctor shook his head. "Absolutely not, Katie. You're a very sick young lady."

Apprehension over missing school and track season was replaced by fear. "How sick?" she heard her father ask.

"Cardiomyopathy is fatal," Dr. Curtis said. "Katie's only real hope is a heart transplant, but getting into the program is complicated."

She learned that getting a heart transplant was a long process that began with interviews for psychological suitability—not everyone who needed a new organ could handle receiving one.

The O'Roarks learned that nationwide, over twenty-five thousand people were awaiting lifesaving transplants, for hearts, kidneys, or livers, and that every four hours, someone died—still waiting. She learned that even if she was eligible, she would be placed on the long waiting list of the university's transplant program.

Her father had demanded to know how she could be moved to the head of the list. Dr. Curtis patiently explained, "Need is our main criteria of evaluation."

"You said Katie needed it. That she'll die without it."

"Right now, she's stable and ambulatory. There are others much sicker. Even if she goes onto the list, she'll have to wait for a suitable donor, one similar in body structure—someone tall and slim with her rare blood type."

"Could her blood type be a drawback?"

"It depends. Sometimes, it can move her to the top of the list, all other factors being equal. Sometimes, it can be an impediment because the rarer the blood type, the harder to match it."

Katie had listened to all the talk and grown more frightened. With so much against her, how did she have a chance? Then, mysteriously, the day before she checked out of the hospital to return home, the letter and the check had arrived from the One Last Wish Foundation. The mysterious JWC's gift had suffused her with new hope. Surely, someone understood her plight. Someone realized how desperate her situation was growing day by day. Although money wasn't a criterion for who received a transplant, she was grateful for the kindness of JWC.

Dr. Curtis sent her home with a regime of medications. Katie did all right for awhile, but now she was bedridden and on oxygen almost twenty-four hours a day. Katie read her Wish letter every day and prayed that she'd live long enough to spend the money from a stranger she could only hope one day to meet.

Two

KATIE WOKE WITH a start. Someone had closed her blinds, and her room was shrouded in gloom. She looked around for Melody, then realized that she must have fallen asleep while her friend had been visiting with her. She imagined Melody tiptoeing out so as not to awaken her, and felt embarrassed. She couldn't even last through a half-hour visit.

From downstairs, she heard the sounds of her mother preparing supper. Sadness stole over her as she remembered how once she would have been setting the table and telling her mom about her day at school. Katie felt tears well up, and she might have allowed them to flow, but her father walked through the doorway.

"Got time for a visit from your old man?" he asked.

Katie quickly wiped away the tears, not wanting him to see her bawling and feeling sorry for herself. "Plenty of time," she told him.

He took the chair Melody had used. "Can I turn on a light?"

"Go ahead. I didn't realize it was so late."

He lit the lamp, and immediately she felt less alone. "How're you doing, honey?"

"I'm sort of down today, Dad." She figured, why lie?

He took her hand, his blue eyes looking pained. "I'd give anything if I could make this all go away for you."

"I know." There had been a time when she'd believed that her daddy could do anything. He was strong and big, with a hearty laugh that had chased away goblins when she was a small child, scared by the dark. "I thought you had to cover a football game tonight," she said.

Since her dad was a sports reporter, autumn was one of his busiest times of the year. He covered area high school football and many of the University of Michigan games in his biweekly column. "I got Hank to fill in for me."

"So you could sit around and watch me sleep?"

"I'm working on other projects this week." He had a computer set up in the den that was linked to the newspaper's main terminal.

"You're not going to do another schmaltzy column about me, are you?"

"Is that what you think of my writing?" He pretended to look offended.

"Only when it's about me." In truth, when he'd written about her last spring, it had been one of the proudest moments of her life. He'd called her "a flash of brilliance" with "wings on her feet, swift enough to bring victory laurels to her school and pride to her father's heart."

"The story I wrote about the need for organ donors has brought a flood of mail in to the paper."

Of course, he was talking about the same story Melody had mentioned. "Sure . . . but did it bring in any hearts?"

He smiled at her dark humor. Her mother entered the room, sat down on Katie's bed, and fussed with the bed sheet. "Supper's on hold," she said. "I thought I'd bring trays up and we could all eat together tonight."

Katie knew something was up, because they both looked so serious. "What's happening, Dad?" she asked.

"I had a powwow with Dr. Curtis and the chief honcho of the transplant department today."

"You didn't cause a scene, did you?"

"I've tried that already, remember? No. Today we talked about your overall condition. You're weaker, Katie. Two weeks ago, you could navigate the stairs if we helped you. And you weren't sucking on oxygen around the clock."

"I don't want to go back to the hospital. I hate it there." Here at home, she at least had all the familiar trappings of her life around her. It was comforting.

"Katie, Dr. Curtis is putting you on a beeper."

Going on the beeper meant that she'd been activated on the United Network for Organ Sharing—UNOS—the national computer network that matches donated organs with waiting patients. "I moved up on the list?" she asked.

"You're a priority, Katie," her mother said.

"The hospital will give us a beeper," her dad explained. "It can go off anytime, day or night. When it does, we go immediately to the hospital, because it means they have a potential donor for you. And as you know, time is of the essence."

Katie felt a fine film of perspiration break out on her face. Living in the same city as a national transplant center made it easier for her to get to the hospital quickly, but the donor heart might be coming from anywhere. And despite all the newest and latest medical technology, a donated organ had maybe a four-hour life span outside the human body. That meant that her surgeons had very little time to transport the heart and place it inside her.

"I guess I should be glad. It's what we've all been waiting for, isn't it?" Katie remarked.

"*I'm* glad," her mother said. "Even though the procedure is risky, it's your only hope."

"Seems weird to be waiting for someone to die so that I can live, doesn't it?"

"Don't think of it that way. Think of it as an opportunity to help a part of somebody live beyond their appointed life span," her dad replied.

"The operation will cost a lot of money, won't it?" Katie changed the subject because the idea of extending someone else's life through herself was too mind-boggling.

"Don't you think one bit about that part, Katie," her mother said. "We can't put a price on your life."

"Use the Wish money."

"My health insurance at work will cover the transplant," her father told her.

Suddenly, Katie's chest tightened and pain shot through her. She was afraid that she might pass out.

Seeing her distress, her mother turned up the valve on the oxygen tank. "Do you need a pain pill?" she asked anxiously.

Katie shook her head. She disliked the dopey feeling the medicine gave her. Instead, she took great gulps of pure oxygen until she felt the pain subside and her head clear.

"Think of something fun you want to do with the money," her mother said, trying to pick up the thread of the conversation. Katie could hear a fearful tremor in her voice. "Your father and I will handle the finances. You pick something exciting for us all to do once this is over and you're better."

Katie gazed around her room to her desk heaped with books, to shelves that held countless ribbons and trophies for field and track events she'd won over the years. "All I want to do is run again," she whispered.

"Even if the transplant's successful, you may not get to do that," her mother said.

Katie couldn't imagine her life without running.

"But if the transplant works, why can't I do everything I always did before? They can't fix me up, then tell me I have to be an invalid for the rest of my life."

"Don't get overly excited, dear. We can talk about the future once you've had your transplant."

"I want to live," Katie persisted, looking at her parents' worried faces. "And for me, living is running. I had a real chance at a college track scholarship before all this happened."

"You'll go to college," her mother declared. "I wouldn't fret about that. You'll discover other things to be interested in, other things to be involved with as you get older."

Katie knew from meetings with the transplant staff that heart transplant patients had a survival rate of eighty-five percent for their first year following the procedure, and a fifty percent chance of living five years. In five years, she'd be twenty-one—of legal age to vote. If she lived . . . if she first survived the surgery.

"Let's not think about what you'll be losing," her father added, sensing her disappointment. "Let's think about what you'll be gaining."

"The chance to live," Katie said. How fickle life could be. Months before, she'd been a regular teenager, a top track star with a lifetime of plans and dreams. Now, because of some complications from a virus, she was struggling to stay alive. Her thoughts turned to her mysterious benefactor, who'd written, ". . . you and I have much in common." Had JWC needed a transplant, too? If so, had he or she gotten it? Had JWC survived? If it had turned out well, then why had JWC chosen to remain anonymous? Didn't JWC realize that a personal visit to prove that all was well was worth more than a cryptic letter?

Katie sighed and glanced at her parents' concerned expressions. "So, we get the beeper and wait for it to go off," she summarized.

"That's right," her father said. "Now, all we can do is wait."

And pray for somebody's heart, Katie added to herself.

Three

"Gramps, hurry up! We don't want to miss the kickoff," Josh Martel said, glancing back over his shoulder at the elderly man shuffling through the crowd behind him.

"Hold your horses," Gramps grumbled, juggling a lap blanket, a program booklet, and a Michigan football pennant. "You're sixteen, and I'm eighty. You can move faster than me, boy."

Josh slowed, purposefully stepping to the older man's side and relieving him of his pennant and folded blanket. "Let me carry this stuff for you."

The two of them made their way to their box seats at the fifty-yard line of the stadium. "Don't see what the big hurry is, anyway. Kickoff's thirty minutes away," Gramps said.

The box seats were chairs, not benches, like the

majority of the stadium where most of the fans sat. "I didn't realize Aaron got us such good seats," Josh said, spreading the blanket across his grandfather's lap. He studied the football players warming up on the field.

"Do you see him?" Gramps asked.

Josh pointed. "That's Aaron. Number nine." He felt an inordinate sense of pride over seeing his older brother dressed in the blue and yellow of the Wolverines. He scanned the program after flipping it open to the team roster. He pointed to his brother's name. "See, Gramps: 'Aaron Martel, Kicker.' He'll be doing the field goals and extra points."

"I know what a kicker does. I'm not senile, you know."

Josh suppressed a smile. The grizzly old man grumbled a lot, but he was pretty cool. There weren't many men his age who would have taken in two teenage brothers on a week's notice. Of course, Aaron had already been accepted to Michigan on football scholarship and was moving to Ann Arbor, anyway; but things had been so bad at home in Indiana that he'd demanded Josh be allowed to come with him. He could live in Ann Arbor with Gramps, Josh had argued, and go to Ann Arbor High. That way, the brothers could see each other often. Gramps had agreed, and their parents had let them go. Otherwise, Josh would still be stuck in his nightmarish home situation.

Josh saw Aaron jog over to the side of the wall and signal for him to come down. "Be right back," Josh said, and bounded down the stadium steps until he was at the wall, looking over at his brother.

"How's he doing?" Aaron asked, glancing toward the old man.

"You know Gramps—he grouses and pretends this is such a drag, but he's really proud. I heard him telling his neighbor that 'his grandson was going to kick some Irish butt in the game today.' " Josh grinned. "Do you think the Notre Dame bench is scared of the hot-shot freshman kicker from Indiana?"

"Terrified," Aaron answered with a grin. "Not as scared as I am, though."

"Come on . . . You had great high school stats. That's why they gave you a scholarship."

"This is the big time, little bro. High school doesn't count for squat. Speaking of that, how do you like your new school?"

Josh shrugged. "It's awfully big, and I still get lost in the halls. I signed up for cross country. It'll help keep me fit till track starts in the spring."

From out on the field, a whistle blew. "I've got to get to the locker room," Aaron said. He shoved his helmet over his dark curly hair and stepped backward. "I'll see you after the game, and maybe you can come over and shoot some pool with me and the guys next week."

"Sounds cool," Josh called. He watched Aaron wave and disappear into a dark tunnel in the concrete side of the stadium wall.

"Good day for a game," Gramps commented as Josh returned to his seat. "Good day for a win."

Josh had to agree that the September day was perfect as he gazed up at the cloudless blue sky. The air was so crystal clear, it sparkled, and cool nights had already tipped the treetops with red and gold. Josh felt a deep sense of satisfaction in knowing that after years of unhappiness, his and Aaron's luck had changed. He was beginning a new life, getting a fresh start—and he was more than ready.

When the starting whistle blew, thousands of fans surged to their feet. Josh yelled for the Michigan Wolverines, but his eyes were on his brother, who booted the football into the opponent's end zone. By the start of the third quarter, Notre Dame was leading by three points, so when Michigan had a chance to tie it up with a field goal, all fans looked to the spectacular freshman kicker. Josh felt his heart pounding as Aaron jogged out onto the field from the sidelines while thousands of voices began to chant his name.

"Here we go," Gramps yelled. "Do us proud, boy."

The team hunched into formation, and Josh leaned forward in anticipation. The ball was snapped to the holder, who steadied it on the tee. Aaron started running forward, then stopped. Suddenly, he grasped his helmet with both hands, staggered backward, and dropped to one knee. From there, he fell to the ground in a heap. The referee blew his whistle as confusion erupted on the field and disorder in the stands.

Josh felt time begin to move in surrealistic sequence. A group of coaches ran out onto the field and surrounded their downed player, shielding him from thousands of curious eyes. Fans gasped and buzzed with questions. The announcer's voice came over the PA system, "Kicker Aaron Martel is down. Official time-out has been called."

"What's wrong?" Gramps asked, snapping through Josh's stupor. "Why's he lying down?"

Josh shook off shocked numbness and felt adrenaline shoot through him. "I'll be back!" he yelled to his grandfather. In several long-legged bounds, he shot down the stadium steps, boosted himself over the wall, and ran across the field. He barely remembered shoving aside the cop who tried to stop him and continued to chase him.

Coming up to the crush of men hovering over Aaron, Josh shouldered his way through. "He's my brother!" he yelled. "Get out of my way! Let me through."

Hands tried to push Josh away, but not before he saw Aaron lying stretched out on the ground, his helmet off, his face ashy gray. Two coaches were giving him artificial respiration, one pumping Aaron's chest, another blowing air into his mouth. Terror coursed through Josh's body.

Strong hands grabbed him and spun him around. "I'm Coach Muller," a broad, heavyset man said. "Let's give our men room to work."

"What's wrong? What's happened to my brother?"

"We don't know. He's being transported to the hospital."

"Hospital! But how'd he get hurt?"

"We're doing all we can, son." Coach Muller's hands rested firmly on Josh's shoulders.

Josh staggered backward, a heavy sweat flooding over him and turning into a biting chill. He didn't need a doctor to tell him that Aaron was in desperate shape. Soon, he heard the wail of an ambulance, then saw more men rush out onto the field, rolling a portable stretcher. One immediately took over the chest massage, and another thrust a bag over Aaron's mouth and began squeezing. Snatches of dialogue floated over the scene.

". . . not breathing . . . IV's started . . . bagged and ready for transport . . ." As the rolling stretcher went past him, one medic held high an IV pouch, which was attached by a long tube to Aaron's arm. Others pumped the bag protruding from Aaron's mouth and pressed repeatedly on his chest.

"Where're you taking him?" Josh cried. His voice sounded raspy, foreign.

Coach Muller pulled on Josh's arm. "Come with me. I'll drive you. Are you alone?"

Josh suddenly remembered his grandfather up in the stands. "No. Gramps—"

Coach Muller interrupted. "Give me your ticket stub, and I'll have the police bring him."

Obediently, Josh went with the coach, through the darkened tunnel, toward the side gate leading to the coaches' parking lot. From far away, he heard the moan of the ambulance's siren. Its forlorn sound faded into the autumn air like a lost and lonely cry.

*   *   *

The emergency room of the small local hospital was practically empty, and a TV set was tuned to the game. A video replay of Aaron crumbling on the field played at regular intervals, and an announcer kept saying, "No word yet about freshman kicker Aaron Martel." Josh stared vacantly at the endless scene, each time feeling anew the horror of watching Aaron fall.

At some point, the police arrived with his grandfather, whose eyes looked confused and watery. The staff showed Josh, Gramps, and Coach Muller to a small anteroom off one of the corridors, where they sat silently.

"What's taking so long?" Josh sprang out of his chair and paced like a caged animal. "It's been over an hour. Shouldn't they know something by now?" He wanted to burst through the doorway and go find Aaron, but the coach restrained him.

"They'll let us know as soon as possible," the coach said soothingly.

Josh heard loud voices in the hallway and realized that the police had sealed off the area. Reporters had already flocked to the hospital.

"Do you think the doctors will be able to find us stuck off here in this little room?" Gramps asked. "Do you think they'll remember where they put us?"

Josh gazed down at the old man, sitting hunched in a chair. He looked small and helpless, and Josh felt a surge of pity for him. He crouched beside Gramps and took his hand. "Do you want something, Gramps? Some coffee? Water?"

Gramps peered hesitantly into Josh's face. "Aaron's a good boy. You tell the doctors that. He doesn't do drugs like some kids. He's a real good boy."

Josh felt a knot form in his throat. He forced it down, replacing his urge to cry with renewed fury. "This waiting is stupid! They can't lock us up in here like this!"

Before he could flee, the door opened and a man dressed in green hospital scrubs came inside. Josh stood, feeling as if all the air had been sucked from the tiny room. "I'm Dr. Wright—the ER physician." Behind his thick glasses, his expression looked haggard and defeated.

"What's wrong? How's Aaron?"

Dr. Wright put his hand on Josh's shoulder. "Your brother's dead, son. He died before he hit the ground."

Four

~~~

"YOU'RE LYING!" THE words exploded out of Josh's mouth. He took a swing at the doctor and might have connected with a punch, but Coach Muller grabbed his arm.

Stunned, the doctor jumped backward. "I'm sorry, but it's true. We've got him on a respirator, and we've completed testing—he's totally unresponsive."

The door opened, and another doctor hurried into the room. "I'm Dr. Lowenstein, a neurologist. Please, let me talk to you."

Josh felt his heart thudding inside his chest like a runaway train. He felt lightheaded and queasy. Dr. Lowenstein took his elbow and guided him over to a chair next to Gramps. "Son, I know how difficult this is for you, and I'd give anything if I could tell you otherwise, but your brother suffered an aneurysm in his brain—a rupture of a major blood vessel."

"Aneurysm?" Gramps interrupted. "That's for old people. Aaron was just a boy."

"I'm positive it was a congenital defect, something he was born with," Dr. Lowenstein explained.

"I don't understand what an aneurysm is," Josh told the doctor. *It's a mistake*, his mind shouted. *A terrible mistake.*

"Picture a garden hose with water rushing through it. Now, imagine there's a bulge in the hose. The more pressure applied by the rushing water, the weaker the bulge becomes, until finally it bursts."

"But he was so healthy. He was a football player, very physical." Coach Muller had come alongside of the trio.

"His physical condition has nothing to do with it. The aneurysm was a time bomb waiting to go off. Nothing could have predicted it. Nothing could have prevented it from happening. I'm sorry."

Josh didn't believe the doctor had a right to be sorry. He didn't even know Aaron. "I want to see my brother," Josh said, standing.

"Of course. He's in Intensive Care." Dr. Lowenstein nodded to Dr. Wright, who opened the door and led the way down the hallway.

They rode up the elevator in silence, got off, and walked down another long corridor to a door marked NEURO ICU. There, Dr. Lowenstein paused and turned to Josh and Gramps. "First, let me tell you what you're going to see. There's a lot of machinery around Aaron. The respirator is breathing for him, a heart monitor is keeping track of his heartbeat, a catheter is helping to eliminate excessive fluids. He *looks* like he's asleep."

"I want to see him," Josh insisted.

Inside the ICU, Josh was aware of nurses and a desk area with beeping monitors. He kept his eyes straight ahead, not wanting to establish eye contact with anyone. He didn't want to be in the room with these people. He wanted to take his brother home to Gramps's. Dr. Lowenstein led the way into a small cubicle. There, on a bed, lay Aaron. A tube protruded from his mouth, held in place by crisscrossed tape. All around him, machines hissed, beeped, and hummed.

Aaron's eyes were closed, and his dark, curly hair looked matted. His skin looked flushed, almost rosy. Josh felt a momentary surge of relief as he remembered Aaron's awful gray color on the field. "Can I touch him?" he asked.

"Of course."

Slowly, Josh walked to the side of the bed, where he reached out and took Aaron's hand. His flesh felt warm, alive. He looked as if any minute he might awake, sit up, and ask what all the fuss was about. The doctors were mistaken, Josh thought. Aaron couldn't possibly be dead.

Gramps shuffled over and stroked Aaron's forehead. "Doesn't seem possible, does it?" he mumbled.

Josh turned toward the doctor. "How can you be sure? How do you know he's really dead?" A hard knot of fear had risen inside him. "What proof have you got? We can't just take your word, you know."

Dr. Lowenstein shook his head. His expression was somber, yet compassionate. "What you're seeing is an illusion of aliveness. Believe me, medicine has some highly accurate criteria for determining death." He counted off on his fingers. "Your brother has no response to external stimuli, no reflex activity—most important, no upper brain activity. He has no brainstem or automatic reflexes, meaning his pupils don't react to light, he has no gag or cough reflex.

"When I was called in, I ordered an EEG to measure higher brain activity. Aaron was a flatline. I also ordered an arterial blood flow X ray. That, too, confirmed that he had no brain activity."

With every word, Josh felt as if nails were being driven into his heart. Aaron looked alive, but every test, every wonder of modern technology said otherwise. "I can't believe it," he said, his voice cracking.

"I've lived too long," Gramps said. "I wish I could trade places with him."

For a moment, Josh wished the same thing for himself. Aaron should be the one to live. He had such potential, a lifetime of plans and dreams. Josh remembered Aaron's telling him, "I'm glad I'm playing football in college. It's my ticket for an education, but I'm no jock. I want the education. I want to do something with my life—be something. I don't want to waste myself the way Pop has."

"I think I need to sit down." Gramps's voice jarred Josh.

"There's a room across the hall. We can sit in there," Dr. Lowenstein suggested. "I'll have some coffee brought in . . . and there's someone who wants to talk to you, a Mrs. Gillespe."

Josh didn't want to talk to anyone. He wanted to stay with Aaron, but he also knew his grandfather needed attention.

The small room looked almost homey, with a sofa and easy chairs. A table was centered between the furniture. When the door opened, Josh looked up to see a pretty woman with short, wispy brown hair. She was carrying a tray filled with sodas and coffee. "I'm Bette Gillespe," she said. "I'm from the Michigan Donor Services."

She handed Josh a cold drink which Josh drank. He hadn't realized how thirsty he'd become. The cold soda revived him. "Thank you," he said.

Dr. Lowenstein sat across from him, next to the woman, and Gramps sagged against the sofa beside Josh. Coach Muller had remained out in the hall to make phone calls. Josh studied Gramps's hands. They looked gnarled and leathery, and they were trembling. Josh fought back tears, determined not to break down in front of these strangers. He knew they were trying to be kind. Numbness carried him along. As long as he could hold his feelings in check, he knew he could make it.

"Dr. Lowenstein has explained Aaron's condition

to you," Bette stated. When Josh nodded, she asked, "You understand what's happened to Aaron?"

"He's gone," Josh replied flatly. "He's never coming back."

"I'm so sorry," she said. "There's no rhyme or reason to any of this. Frankly, you'll be sorting it out for the rest of your life. Yet, even though you're hurting right now, I want to offer you an option that may help bring something positive out of this tragedy."

"An option?"

"Did Aaron ever discuss organ donation with you?"

It dawned on Josh then what this meeting was really all about. He recoiled. "Is that what you want? You want us to give Aaron's insides to medical science?"

"Not to medical science," Mrs. Gillespe said quickly. "To suffering, dying people. People who have no other hope to live except through the generosity of grieving families such as yours. The gift of an organ for transplantation—of Aaron's organs—can turn a sick, hopeless person into a functioning, vital human being again."

"What's she saying?" Gramps asked, leaning forward. "She wants us to say it's all right to cut Aaron up?"

"There will be no disfigurement," Mrs. Gillespe assured them. "Top surgeons remove only the organs you wish to donate, and they leave your loved one looking perfectly normal."

Josh was listening to his grandfather's objections, but he was also recalling the time when he and Aaron had been watching some TV show about a girl hooked to life-support machinery and a family demanding that the machines be turned off. Aaron had said, "Man, I'd never want to be kept alive that way. If I go first, little bro, you make sure I don't lie around like some vegetable. And before you put me in the ground, pass around my best parts." He had laughed, made a face, and added, "Like Frankenstein, I'll rise from the dead."

Guiltily, Josh glanced down at the floor. He *knew* what Aaron would have wanted. Still, hearing Gramps's protestations made Josh pause. Gramps was saying, "We can't afford no fancy surgeons."

"You would pay nothing to donate Aaron's organs for transplantation. You'd pay only for the care he's had thus far."

Dr. Lowenstein said, "Because Aaron had heart-chest massage from the moment his aneurysm occurred, his blood was kept flowing. That means his organs are in excellent condition. Plus, he was young and healthy. Many people could benefit from your gift of Aaron."

"Who would get his organs? Would we know?" Josh asked.

"Probably not," Mrs. Gillespe said, "although the trend to keep donors and recipients apart is changing. Research is finding that often such knowledge is beneficial to both parties. If the family of a donor ever gets to meet someone who's received a loved one's organ, they feel blessed.

"For the most part, however, donors and their families don't know the recipients. The organs are matched by computer with people on a waiting list. Every effort is made to place an organ in the immediate area, at least within the state. But donor and recipient must be matched by medical urgency, blood type, time on the waiting list—" She paused. "All those factors have to be considered."

"You didn't just let Aaron die so you could get his organs, did you?" Gramps blurted out.

Josh could see how confused and upset he'd gotten. Josh reached over and took his arm. "Take it easy, Gramps."

Five

❦

"I'M NOT INVOLVED with the organ transplant program," Dr. Lowenstein explained calmly. "I called Mrs. Gillespe because I'm a physician who strongly believes in organ transplantation, and the trauma around Aaron's death makes him an ideal candidate."

"The decision belongs to the family," Mrs. Gillespe said. "Please consider letting something positive come out of this terrible tragedy. For Aaron's sake, for yours, for all the people he can help with a gift of life."

"We should call your mother," Gramps said slowly to Josh. Then, turning to the others, he explained, "My daughter . . . Aaron's her son."

"No." Josh shook his head firmly. "You're our legal guardian, Gramps. She probably wouldn't be sober enough to decide what to do, anyway." He looked over at Mrs. Gillespe. "How much time do we have to decide?"

"Unfortunately, time is our enemy. Once brain death occurs, deterioration of a body and its vital organs is rapid. The machines are keeping Aaron going for now, but we should act quickly."

Josh felt torn, as if he were two people—a sixteen-year-old boy who was losing his brother, and a grown man who was being asked to make a decision no one should have to make. He looked to his grandfather. "It's up to us, Gramps. You and me. We have to decide."

The old man nodded. "I suppose it is. I didn't ever expect it to come to something like this when I said I'd be responsible for you and Aaron. I wish Gran was here." His voice sounded raspy. "She'd know what to do. You've known Aaron all your life, Josh. I've just really come to know him recently. Do you know what he would have wanted us to do?"

Josh covered his eyes. The light in the room seemed too bright, and it was giving him a headache. *Aaron, what should I do?* he pleaded silently. *Help me.* Aaron had always been there for him, shielding him, standing up for him when their father had come home drunk and mean. It had been Aaron who was always in the stands cheering for him when he ran track. Aaron, who'd been his true family. But now, Aaron was leaving him alone with this heavy decision.

Josh lowered his hand and looked directly at

Gramps. "He would have wanted us to donate his organs, because that's the kind of person he was. He put others first."

Gramps hunched his shoulders, and Josh saw a tear trickle down the old man's face. Afraid he'd come unglued himself, Josh stood abruptly. "Can I see Aaron again?"

"Certainly. Take your time. I know how difficult it is to say good-bye."

At the door, Josh paused. "When will you start . . . you know . . . taking out his organs?"

"We'll put the call out immediately with all Aaron's vital statistics. When a donor match is found, a transplant team will be dispatched here. We'll take him upstairs and begin prepping him for organ harvesting this evening."

Organ harvesting. To Josh, the phrase sounded like some kind of primitive farming ritual. "I'm not sure I want everyone to know what we've decided."

"You can decide whether to tell others or not."

"We'll want to have a funeral," Gramps said. "So we can say a proper good-bye."

"Don't worry—the hospital and the university will work with you to make arrangements," Mrs. Gillespe said. "Thank you so very much. What you've decided to do today will help many people."

Josh walked out of the room and back to Neuro ICU. Once inside the cubicle, he bent over his brother's body. Mesmerized, he watched Aaron's chest rise and fall in perfect cadence with the respirator. On the screen of the monitor, he studied the ragged green line as it moved in perfect harmony with the machine. Tentatively, he placed the palm of his hand on Aaron's chest. Through the thin material of the hospital gown, Josh could feel the thumping of his brother's heart.

The sensation was supposed to mean *life*. In Aaron's case, it meant only an imitation of life. Aaron's body may have been stretched out on the bed, but his spirit, his consciousness, was far removed from this time and place. "Hey, bro," Josh whispered, using the term Aaron had often used for Josh. "I guess this is it. I tried to do the right thing by you with this donation business, because I was pretty sure it's what you would have wanted."

Josh kept his hand on Aaron's chest, afraid to break off this final connection. "I don't know when I'll see you again, but I will," he added. His voice broke, and despite all his efforts to remain in control, sobs came quickly, silently. All at once, the walls of the room seemed to be moving in on him, and Josh knew he had to get outside into the cold autumn air. He had to leave this room of death, leave this body, which looked like his brother in form and substance, but really was no more than an elaborate mannequin.

Josh bent, kissed Aaron's forehead, and fled the room.

"Katie! Katie, wake up! The beeper's gone off." Her father's urgent voice sounded as if it were coming from a long way off. Katie struggled toward it, like a swimmer exhaustedly treading water.

Her eyes blinked open as she took long gulps of pure oxygen. "My beeper?" she mumbled.

"They've found you a heart, honey, and the doctors want us at the hospital immediately."

Her parents bundled her up and switched her to a portable oxygen tank. She carried it in her lap, even after they arrived at the hospital and placed her in a wheelchair. Time blurred as she passed from procedure to procedure, area to area. In order to keep her mind off the ordeal awaiting her, she focused on small things—the feel of her mother's hand on hers, the changing of her clothes to hospital issue, the smiles of staff, nurses, doctors, technicians, and orderlies. She half heard their explanations of preparation for her surgery. She felt the pricks of needles and the excruciating pain of the first injection of immune-suppressant drugs in her thigh muscle. She knew that she'd be taking immune-suppressant medications for the rest of her life once her new heart was in place. Fortunately, most came in pill form.

At one point, she heard her father ask Dr. Jacoby, the transplant surgeon, "Who's the donor?"

The doctor answered, "I don't know. Only that he was a young man who died suddenly and unexpectedly. His organs were in outstanding condition. Katie's getting his heart, a boy in Detroit is getting his liver, and his kidneys are on the way to Chicago and Indiana."

Katie tuned out the conversation. She didn't

want to know . . . couldn't bear the idea that someone's body parts were being flown all over the country, even if it was to save lives like hers. Yet, she was grateful, too. Unspeakably grateful.

Orderlies rolled her on a stretcher down the hall toward the operating rooms. Her parents walked on either side. Her mother's face looked pasty, and although Katie was groggy from her preop medications, she was concerned for her mom. Her dad looked less pale, but she could tell by the iciness of his fingers as they gripped hers that he wasn't handling what was happening with ease.

At the door of one of the ORs, the stretcher stopped. "This is as far as your family can go, Katie," Dr. Jacoby said. "There's a waiting room down the hall for them."

"How long?" her mother asked.

"The surgery takes around four hours."

Katie saw her dad slip his arm around his wife's shoulders. "We'll be waiting."

They bent over Katie. "I'll be praying for you, baby," her mother whispered. Katie heard a quiver in her voice.

"I love you both so much," Katie told them. Her tongue felt thick, difficult to move.

"You're a winner, Katie," her father said. "You've been a winner all your life, and this time you're running the ultimate race. You'll win it, too."

Katie was certain she saw tears in his eyes. "Thanks, Daddy." She held up her fingers in a V-for-victory sign. "One more thing," Katie whispered. "If something goes wrong in there, please do something special with my Wish money."

"You'll be spending that money yourself," her dad insisted. "Every penny of it."

Katie wanted to tell her parents a hundred other things, but her brain felt fuzzy, and it was growing harder to think straight, much less put her thoughts into words. She was afraid that once she was rolled inside the OR, she'd never see them again. The door to the OR swung open, and a nurse dressed in green scrubs and a mask said, "We're ready."

Katie clutched her mother's hand. She wanted to scream, "*I'm not.*" She heard her mother say, "See you in a few hours. We love you so much."

Katie was shuttled into the OR, helplessly watching her parents' beloved faces until the door swung shut, closing them out. The operating room was so bright, it hurt her eyes. She caught glimpses of machines and stainless steel tables. She was lifted onto a cold table. Dr. Jacoby leaned over her. "We're going to give you a brand new heart, Katie," he said through his mask. "I know this is scary for you, but my team and I've done this operation many times before, and we're really pretty darn good at it.

"As I've explained, we'll put you to sleep, cool your body temperature, and put you on the heart-lung machine." He gestured toward a large piece of gray-and-blue machinery. "Then I'll take out the old and put in the new.

"When you wake up, you'll be in the recovery room. You'll have tubes coming out of your chest and out of your mouth. You won't be able to talk until we remove the breathing tube, which should be on day two of your recovery. Don't be alarmed. The tubes will be pulled as soon as you're stabilized."

His eyes crinkled above his mask. "You'll be in isolation for the first few days—there are lots of nasty germs floating around, and we don't want you to catch any of them. You'll be able to see your parents and, of course, me." He smiled again. "You're going to do just fine, Katie."

Heart-lung machines, tubes, isolation—the terms swirled around in her head. "How will I know if I'm alive?" Katie asked, in a fit of dark humor.

He laughed. "You'll *feel* alive. At first, you'll feel as if a freight train ran over you but you'll have an immediate awareness that you're better. Your fingernails will turn pink again, and you won't need oxygen in order to breathe. It's like falling in love, Katie—you'll just *know*."

She gazed up at him. "Then let's get moving."

"Hi. I'm Max, your anesthesiologist. I'm slipping some 'happy juice' into your IV, then I'll put this little rubber mask over your face. Breathe deep and try to count to ten. I bet you won't make it to four."

Katie could feel a numbness stealing over her body from the IV dripping into her hand. She suddenly felt light, weightless, as if she were floating right off the table. "See you in recovery, Katie," Max said. "Sweet dreams."

In recovery, Katie thought silently, as she felt the rubber mask being placed over her mouth and nose. *Or in heaven.*

Six

KATIE DRIFTED ON a luxurious sea of warmth like a piece of wood coasting on ocean waves. Voices came and went; she could hear them, but she couldn't make out what they were saying. She didn't care. The water felt so blissful, so peaceful, she never wanted to leave it.

A bright light came toward her, hovering above her face as she lay stretched out in the water. The light began to take on a form. It shimmered and dissolved into a being of incredible beauty. "Who are you?" Katie asked.

"I'm JWC," the being said.

"You are?" Katie felt a surge of delight. "You gave me the money!"

"It was nothing. It was for your heart."

"I haven't got a heart."

"I know. You're like the Tin Man from The Wizard of Oz—*no heart."*

"The Wizard gave him a heart."

The beautiful creature laughed. "Not at all. I gave him a heart."

"You did? But in the movie—"

"Whoops! Got to go."

Katie tried to touch the beautiful being, but her arms felt pinned. "No. Don't leave me!" Katie cried.

"Can't stay. I have money to give away. Hearts to buy."

Katie watched the phantom JWC recede and felt an overwhelming sense of panic. "Don't go! Please!"

The light moved away from her and started growing brighter. Katie tried to close her eyes, because suddenly the light was so bright, it burned her eyeballs. There was a terrible crushing sensation in her chest. She gasped, struggled to breathe, reached out her hand toward the light, the way a drowning person grabs for a lifeline.

". . . wake up, Katie. It's all over, little girl. Come on, wake up and give Max a smile."

Katie opened her eyes. She saw the anesthesiologist's face. She tried to speak, but a tube down her throat prevented her.

"It's okay, sweetheart," Max said. "I'm only giving you your wake-up call. You came through with flying colors, Katie. Your new heart's in place and working fine."

She squeezed her eyes shut, afraid she was having another dream. Her chest felt heavy, as if lead weights were pressing against it. She heard a constant blip-blip sound from a nearby machine.

Max continued talking. "You'll have lots of nurses watching over you—little guardian angels. We'll move you down to ICU in a few hours. Meanwhile, I've got two very anxious parents on my hands. Think you're up to seeing them for a few minutes?"

Katie opened her eyes. She wanted to nod, but wasn't positive she could pull off the movement.

"I'll bring them in," Max said. He straightened up, then paused. "First, let me show you something." He picked up her hand, the one not attached to an IV, and held it in front of her face. "What do you see?" he asked.

Katie blinked, attempting to focus. The light from over her bed shone clearly on her hand. With wonder, she saw that her fingertips were a healthy, rosy shade of glowing pink.

Josh felt as if the whole world had turned upside down. The entire University of Michigan football team, the coaches, staff members, and some faculty were standing outside in the grayness of the September afternoon around his brother's coffin. The players should have been on a football field, not here in a cemetery. Some of the boys were crying openly, which jarred Josh. Here were these big, strapping mountains of muscle and sinew, weeping like babies. He thought it strange.

He himself was red-eyed from unshed tears. He stood beside his grandfather, holding the old man's arm, shoring him up. Josh stared helplessly at the bronze-color coffin, at the mantel of maize and blue mums and carnations draped across it. Aaron was dead. Gone forever. Josh's mind could scarcely grasp the enormousness of such a time span. *Forever.*

Before the funeral, Coach Muller had told Josh and Gramps, "Don't worry about the cost of this. The university will pay the tab. Aaron was on athletic scholarship, and he was insured. We'll see to it that he has a fine funeral."

Josh had wanted to shout, *Who cares?* He'd wanted to hit something with his fists. He'd wanted to throw a chair through the plate-glass window of the funeral home. But he'd done nothing, because the funeral ritual was important to his grandfather.

"Flowers are nice," he heard Gramps mutter. "Gran had real nice flowers at her funeral, too. Aaron's with her now—do you know that, Josh? The two of them are together."

Josh had to bite back an angry retort. Gran was in the ground, and Aaron was in a coffin soon to go in the ground. They were both dead. "Sure, Gramps. Whatever you say."

After the ceremony, they all went to his grandfather's small house, where neighbors had brought in food. Josh moved like a zombie through the clusters of mourners. As he passed by, one of the players reached out and took his arm. "Remember me?" he asked.

"You're Dion. One of Aaron's roommates."

"I'm really sorry, man. Your brother was a good guy."

"Thanks."

"Did your folks come?"

For a moment, Josh didn't know how to respond.

"Aaron leveled with me about them," Dion said. " 'Cause my old man's a drunk, too."

Josh clenched his fists, trying not to feel bitter as he said, "No. They couldn't make it. Pop's in jail for driving under the influence of his usual booze, and Mom's in the hospital. He beat her up pretty bad before the cops picked him up."

"That stinks, man."

"Life stinks," Josh said, then left the room.

It seemed like hours before everybody left. Josh stayed in his room, lying on his bed, staring up at the ceiling until it was dark. From below, he heard the woman from next door directing others about cleaning up. He heard Gramps climb the creaking stairs and rap softly on the bedroom door. He wished the old man would go away. He didn't want to talk to anyone.

Gramps came inside, uninvited, and lowered himself slowly to the side of Josh's bed. "You all right?" he asked.

"Sure. Just fine."

Gramps placed his wrinkled hand on Josh's shoulder. "I know how you're hurting, boy. I've been down this road before."

Josh wanted to say, *No one knows how bad I hurt*, but he didn't. Gramps said, "When Gran died, I wanted to crawl into that casket with her. I didn't figure that I could make it without her. We'd been married forty-five years, you know."

Go away, Josh pleaded silently.

"But I have made it for about seven years now. They haven't been easy years . . . especially the first one, but I've made it. And you will, too. The hurt goes away—the raw hurt, the angry hurt."

Josh felt his throat constrict.

"You know, there was a spell when I was downright mad at her for dying on me." Josh's gaze darted to Gramps's face. "That's right," Gramps affirmed, seeing the look. "Just plain mad. She had no right to go off and leave me to muddle through the rest of my life alone. No right at all."

"What am I going to do?" Josh's voice was barely a whisper. "He was my only brother."

"Same thing I did. You're going to go on living." Gramps spoke slowly, as if hunting for the words. "You've got a lot of living ahead of you, son. A lot that Aaron would have wanted you to do. You don't have to start back to school right away if you don't want, but you can't stop going altogether, either."

"I don't care about school."

"And track?"

"I don't care about that anymore."

"You care," Gramps said. "Maybe not right this moment, but you care. Just the way Aaron cared about football. Nothing's going to bring him back, nothing's going to stop the aching you feel—except time. One day, the ache will be duller. Don't stay mad at the world, or at God, for the rest of your life. You'll only eat yourself away from the inside out."

Gramps's words fell on Josh like cold rainwater. The wound was too new, too fresh. He couldn't pretend he didn't hate heaven and earth. What kind of a universe was it when someone like Aaron got leveled in the prime of his life? What had Aaron ever done to deserve an artery's going haywire in his brain? "Aaron was only twenty years old," Josh said. "Nothing about what's happened makes any sense."

"It never will," Gramps said. "You'll make yourself crazy trying to figure it out. Life happens— good and bad. Folks don't always get what they deserve, either way. I can tell you this, though—a person never grows deep unless he's been through suffering. Seems strange that pain and suffering become the soil of strength and courage, but that's the way it works."

Josh wanted to shout that he and Aaron both had seen their share of suffering, and that what was happening now seemed punitive and cruel.

"The ones who are left behind have to pick up the pieces and go on, because that's just what the living do. We go on living," Gramps continued. "I know you won't believe me, but one day, you'll be happy again. That's one of the hardest things to catch hold of when you're hurting real bad. Just the way bad things happen, good things happen, too. Make a life for yourself . . . Aaron would have wanted you to."

Josh turned toward the wall, saying nothing.

The old man patted Josh's shoulder. "I'm going to turn in. I wish I could help you more, son. I wish I could stop your hurting."

Gramps shuffled out of the room, and Josh stared at the blank wall. He felt as if his insides were on fire. He clutched his arms to himself, trying to hold back the storm of emotions building within him. He'd given away Aaron's heart, and now he felt as if there were a void inside his own chest. "Please . . . please, Aaron, don't leave me. Please." The words poured out of Josh like a litany. Reason told him that Aaron was gone and no amount of chanting would change it. Still, he couldn't stem the flow of words that began to mingle with large, racking sobs as he lay in the dark.

Seven

W‍HEN THEY PULLED out the breathing tube after surgery and Katie could talk again, she felt euphoric. Her voice sounded hoarse, and her throat ached, but the sense of relief she felt was overwhelming. "I made it, Mom, Dad," she told her parents after she'd been moved from recovery into isolation.

"I told you, you're a winner," her dad said. All she could see of his face were his eyes and eyebrows above his mask.

Her mother couldn't stop touching her. "You're beautiful, Katie, beautiful. You look so healthy."

Katie didn't have the courage to look in a mirror, but she knew that she was better. Every beat of the heart now lying in her chest sent fresh, oxygenated blood pouring through her. Also, without being tethered to an oxygen tank, she felt an incredible sense of freedom, even though all Dr. Jacoby would let her do was sit up on the edge of the bed.

"So soon?" her mother asked anxiously when Dr. Jacoby announced his intentions on Katie's second day out of surgery.

"We've found that getting patients up as quickly as possible is to their benefit," the doctor said. "We don't want pneumonia to develop."

He and the nurses helped Katie sit upright amid the tangle of tubes and wires. She was woozy, and her chest felt as if it had been struck by a sledge-hammer.

"We'll take the tubes out tomorrow, and you can take a stroll around the room," he promised. "By the end of the week, you should be out of isolation and in a private room."

True to his word, four days later, Dr. Jacoby gave orders for Katie's chest tubes to be pulled. She was completely unhooked from all the machines, the IVs, and the monitors, and moved into a spacious, sunny room.

"When can I go home? When can I go back to school?" she asked when Dr. Jacoby entered her room for rounds.

"You do feel good, don't you?" The doctor laughed, then glanced at her parents. "We won't be able to keep this one down, will we?"

Her father shrugged. "I never could."

Dr. Jacoby's expression grew serious. "Katie, I don't want you to think you're completely out of the woods yet."

"What do you mean?"

"First of all, you've had major surgery. That in itself is reason enough to take things slowly. Second, you've got a new heart. Now, as much as your body needs it to function, as far as your immune system's concerned, this heart is a foreign object."

"I thought that's why I'm taking pills and shots—to turn off my immune system."

"That's right, but expect to go through an episode of rejection. We've done enough of these transplants to know that most recipients do. We'll keep doing tests and giving you the suppressant drugs, but it'll take awhile for your body to adjust."

The thought that her own body might force a shutdown of her new heart made Katie panic. Another heart might not come along if this one was rejected. "I'll do exactly what you tell me," Katie declared. "I want this heart to work."

Dr. Jacoby patted her shoulder. "You and the heart are both young and healthy. We have every reason to believe that you'll do just fine. I only want to alert you that it may not all be smooth sailing."

When he had gone, Katie asked her parents, "You think I'll be all right, don't you?"

"Absolutely," her dad replied. Her mother didn't look as confident, yet she nodded in agreement.

"I had a dream during the operation," Katie said, to change the subject. The notion of rejection was too frightening to dwell on right then. "I dreamed I met JWC. She told me she'd helped the Tin Man in *The Wizard of Oz* find a new heart and that the Wish money had bought my new one."

"So, your dream revealed that JWC is a girl," her father teased. "That's more than I could find out. But as for the money's buying the heart, you know that could never happen. Donors and organs have to be specifically matched."

"I know," Katie said. "It was just such a crazy dream, that's all."

"It was only a dream," her mother said.

"I've wondered about the donor. Do you know anything about who it was?"

"They've told us very little. Why, we don't even know where he was from," her dad answered.

"I was thinking about the donor's family . . ."

"Don't," her mother said quickly. "Just think about getting well."

Katie wanted to talk about it with someone. She wanted to try to deal with an overwhelming tide of emotions that kept sneaking up on her. Who was her donor? How was his or her family dealing with their loss? Their loss was her gain. Someone had died in order to give her life. If only she could tell them "Thank you." The phrase sounded inadequate. Maybe she could do something wonderful for them with her Wish money if she ever discovered their identity.

"You look as if you're a million miles away," her mother said, interrupting Katie's jumbled thoughts.

She looked so anxious that Katie decided not to say anything about what she'd been thinking. "Have you heard from Melody?" she asked.

"I talk to her once a day," her mom said. "She's very eager to talk to you."

"Now that I'm in a room, don't you think she could come see me?"

"Oh, no. It's too soon," her mother blurted out.

"Too soon?"

"What your mom means is that we don't want you exposed unnecessarily to any germs," her father said smoothly.

Katie glanced at their faces. "That's why I'm taking the cyclosporine, isn't it? And the steroids." A thought made her pause. "Do you think that my being on steroids will keep me from running in high school track? I mean, steroids are illegal, but it's not my fault I have to take them."

"Running?" her mother gasped, looking horrified. "Katie, you can't think about running."

Katie blinked. "Why not? My new heart is fine, and so am I. I told you before the operation that I planned to run again."

"We don't need to discuss this now," her father interrupted. "You're barely out of surgery. Do as your doctor says, honey. Rest, take it easy for a while."

Katie wanted to tell them that she'd spent the last four months of her life resting. She felt like a million dollars, compared with how she'd felt before the operation, when every breath had hurt, every movement had left her gasping. "I'll talk to Dr. Jacoby about it," Katie said, attempting to erase the panicked expression on her mother's face. "Will that be okay?"

"Of course." Her mom nodded vigorously, yet Katie could tell she was only humoring her.

That night, she called Melody on the phone. The moment she said hello, Melody burst into tears. "I can't believe it's you."

"I got a new heart, not a new personality," Katie joked, but she did wonder if the new heart might make her different somehow.

"I couldn't believe it," Melody said. "The other day, I came by your house after school, the way I always do, and nobody was there. Turned out you'd gone to the hospital at four o'clock that morning to get a heart transplant! I freaked out. I mean, it was all over, and I hadn't even known you'd gone! Of course, I've been calling your mom daily, and your dad did one of his famous columns about your operation and all, but I felt so cut off from you."

"Dad did another story about me?"

"Don't sound so annoyed. It was really good. I cry every time I read it."

"I wish he wouldn't do that," Katie said.

"But he should," Melody countered. "You're a medical marvel, and your story is so inspiring. I wish everybody could read it." Melody sniffed. "Are you sure you're all right?"

"I'm fine," Katie replied, not truly sure how she was. "As soon as I can get my doctor and my parents to agree, please come see me."

"I will. I can't wait. I've missed you so much, Katie." Melody was still crying when they hung up.

Katie chewed her lower lip thoughtfully. She hadn't realized how profoundly her transplant was going to affect everyone. Her parents, her friends—

everybody seemed to be struggling to come to terms with it. Didn't they realize that she was the one who'd gone through it?

She wished her father hadn't written about it. It was her private life. She didn't want people to go around talking about her as though she were some kind of wonder. She just wanted to get well, go home, and start living a normal life. She hadn't asked to become a medical marvel. Without warning, Katie started to cry. Why had this happened to her? *Why?*

Josh's hands were trembling, and his heart pounded against his rib cage. He felt as if he'd run a marathon. He wet his lips and stared down again at the newspaper spread out on the kitchen table. Quickly, he reread the sports column by Daniel O'Roark.

> *How does a man go about thanking science for the miracle of giving Katie life? This was not a simple surgery to correct a flawed heart. Rather, a surgeon's skilled hands gave our Katie a brand-new heart.*
>
> *Yet, there's more than one player in the drama of my daughter's rebirth. Yes, her surgeon was helpful. Yes, the hospital where she's staying is sustaining her. However, they are but bit players in this drama.*

The story went on to outline the dramatic details of the call that had come in the night to announce that a donor—lost in his youth to a hemorrhage in his brain—had been found. It told of the rush to the hospital, the wait for the completion of the operation, days in recovery and ICU. Josh devoured every detail.

The real hero is the nameless donor, his family, his gift of life . . . his very heart. To help a loved one, someone you know and care about, is one thing. But to help a stranger, a girl you've never met, who may have had only days to live, is the ultimate in human compassion. My regular readers have followed Katie's story over the years, from the time she was born (yes, in typical fatherly pride, I devoted a column to that miracle, too), to now, when she's been reborn.

This is for you, Katie—my daughter, my love.

And this is for you, donor—giver of life. Because of you, my Katie's alive.

Josh stopped reading. Moisture had filled his eyes, along with a sense of unspeakable joy. He knew beyond a shadow of a doubt where Aaron's heart lay. It rested within one Katie O'Roark. And he was equally positive that outside of some impersonal medical computer system, he was the only person who realized it.

Eight

"KATIE, ARE YOU sure you want to do this?"

"Yes, Mom. Please help me." Katie was determined to make it into the bathroom adjoining her private room for a good, long look at herself in the mirror. She knew she'd lost weight. She could feel her ribs and collarbone jutting through the hospital gown she wore. Yet, her hands looked puffy and her face felt fuller.

"Now, you know that the immune-suppressant drugs—the steroids—are making your face look rounded," her mother warned as she helped Katie shuffle toward the bathroom.

"I know what Dr. Jacoby told me," Katie insisted. "I still want to see."

Nervously, Katie positioned herself in front of the mirror. Her mother flipped on the light. Katie stared at the face in the glass and grimaced. "I look awful . . . like a pumpkinhead. And my arms look like two sticks."

"The doctors call it 'moonface,' " her mother explained, still holding Katie's arm for balance. "It will go away when they adjust your cortisone dosage. And once you come home, I'll fatten you up again."

Katie tried to not act too disappointed, but wistfully recalled her once trim, athletic body. "I look weird. Totally weird." She tipped her chin and turned semi-profile, studying her reflection from different angles. "If I had a tan, I'd look like a moon pie."

Her mother smiled. "You're silly. The steroids are supposed to help ward off rejection, you know. So, what does it matter how it makes you look?"

"I hope it's gone before I return to school. No one will know me."

"I'm sure it will be. Are you ready to get back into bed?"

Katie gently tugged her arm away from her mother and hung onto the sink. "Not yet." She reached behind her neck with one hand and gave a tug to the strings holding her hospital gown in place.

"Katie, don't look." Her mother grabbed at the gown to keep it up.

"I just want to see—" Katie's voice stopped midsentence as the gown slid off her shoulders and down to the floor. Her eyes grew wide with horror as she stared at herself in the mirror. She saw a ragged-looking wound, vivid red, held together by black sutures that stretched from the lower part of her neck down the middle of her chest, all the way to her abdomen. She recoiled, and cried, "My God! Look at me! What have they done? Why did you let them do this to me?"

Her mother grasped Katie's shoulders and turned her away from the mirror. "They saved your life, Katie. There was no other way."

Katie's mind reeled. For the first time, she understood exactly what the transplant team had done to her. The doctors had opened up her body, spread apart her rib cage, and cut out her heart. In her mind's eye, she saw a bizarre image of a turkey being prepared for a meal—hollowed out, all its innards removed. She saw the empty cavity refilled with bread stuffing. That's what they'd done—cut her open, ripped out the old, stuffed in the new. Now, they were pumping her full of medicine so that all her new stuffing wouldn't be rejected and fall out.

She wondered about her old heart—the one she'd been born with. What had they done with the poor, diseased thing? Did they throw it away, the way her mother tossed out turkey giblets? She felt sick to her stomach.

"I'm a freak! I'm grotesque!" Katie gaped, wide-eyed, at the long scar.

"No, baby, no. The scar will fade. I promise you. In a few months, it'll be a thin white line."

"No one will ever want to touch me. I'll never be

able to wear a bathing suit again. I'm hideous, ugly." Katie was sobbing, unable to control herself.

Her mother hastily retied the hospital gown and managed to get Katie back into bed. "I'm calling the nurse," she said, pressing the call button. "You're overwrought. It's not good."

"Overwrought! How can you say that? Just look at what they did to me! They sawed me open! They poked around inside me! They've put me back together with staples and glue. They should have let me die."

"Don't ever say that. It's only a scar."

A nurse came hurrying into the room. Katie buried her face—her ugly moonface—in her hands and wept. She heard her mom and the nurse whispering, heard the nurse say things like, "typical reaction" and "postoperative depression." Katie didn't care what they called it. She'd seen with her own eyes what a freak she'd become. She felt violated, abused, and ruined.

The nurse left, then returned and gave her a shot. Minutes later, her tears subsided as a drugged sleep stole over her.

"May I help you?"

Josh gazed down at the hospital receptionist, momentarily stumped by her question. Around him, people bustled past toward banks of elevators for hospital visiting hours. "I . . . uh . . . was wondering what room Katie O'Roark is in."

The woman typed the name on the computer terminal. Josh shoved his hands into the back pocket of his jeans and shifted nervously, telling himself, *You're stupid, man. This whole idea is stupid.* The receptionist glanced up at him. "She's in room 906, but she can't have visitors."

"Oh." Josh felt keenly disappointed.

"Is there something else I can help you with?"

Josh shook his head. "Does it say when she might be able to have visitors?"

"No. Sorry."

"No problem."

"I can take a message from you and see that it's delivered to her room."

Josh stepped backward, suddenly losing his nerve. "That's all right. I'll . . . I'll just check back in a few days." He turned before the receptionist could say anything else and hurried to the front door. He stopped long enough to catch his breath, calm his pounding heart, and rethink his strategy.

"This was dumb," he muttered under his breath. He should have known he wouldn't get in to see her. Even if he had gotten in, what would he have said? *"Hi. You don't know me, but you're using my brother's heart."* Josh shook his head, trying to clear his thoughts.

True, it hadn't been smart for him to come, but ever since he'd read Mr. O'Roark's column about his daughter's transplant, he couldn't get it out of his mind. He thought about it every waking hour, and had even dreamed about it the night before. He'd dreamed of coming to the hospital, going into a room, and seeing Aaron sitting up in a hospital bed.

Aaron had grinned at him, waved, and said, "Hey, bro. What took you so long to come and see me?"

Josh had said, "I thought you were dead. I thought they took out your organs and gave them to dying people."

"They did. But what the people who received my organs don't know is that over time, they turn into *me*."

In the dream, Josh had felt so joyful that he'd rushed across the room and thrown his arms around his brother. He'd awakened, his face damp with tears, alone in his bedroom, in the dark. The feeling of elation slipped away, and melancholia washed over him. The dream had been so real, he could recall the feel of Aaron's body weight against him.

So, right after school, he'd driven the old car that he'd inherited from Aaron to the hospital, only to be told that Katie O'Roark couldn't have visitors. Josh walked out to the car, got in, and slumped against the seat. He felt so lonely. "I miss you, Aaron," he said aloud.

He stared up at the hospital building, rising into the somber October sky. Somewhere on the ninth floor there was a part of Aaron. He wanted . . . *needed* to see Katie, who sheltered Aaron's heart within her body. If only he could see her, touch her, it might bring Aaron back to him in some small way. With a sigh, Josh rubbed his eyes, started the car, and drove slowly out of the parking lot.

*   *   *

"Your mother tells me you had a bad day," Dr. Jacoby said as he stood beside Katie's bed that evening.

She said nothing, only turned her back and huddled down under the covers.

"This kind of reaction isn't unusual, you know. Your body's gone through a big transition, and so have your emotions. I'm going to send in the psychiatrist you met when you and your parents talked about your suitability for the donor program."

"You think I'm crazy?" Katie asked.

"No. Actually, I think you're adjusting very well, but you need to talk about your feelings. You need to get them out in the open." He lifted her chin with his forefinger. "Katie, you've got a long road ahead of you, and a lot to learn about managing your own health. No one can do it for you—you'll be completely in charge."

"In charge, how?" Katie asked.

"You'll be taking immune-suppressant medications for the rest of your life. They must be taken at exact prescribed times, and you can't ever miss a dose. Not one."

Katie glared at him. It sounded as if the schedule controlled her, not vice versa. The serious expression on his face caused angry words about the stifling prospects of her life to die in her throat. He continued, "You'll learn how to monitor your own vital signs—take your temperature and pulse, listen to your heartbeat. You'll come in every three months for a heart biopsy. You'll adhere to a strict diet and an exercise regime."

Exercise. At last, he'd said something she wanted to hear. "What kind of exercise?"

"You'll start slowly, but build up to as much as you can handle."

"Before all this happened, I was a runner," she said cautiously.

"After you're all healed, you may be a runner again."

Katie felt a surge of hope. "That's what I want."

"Tomorrow, I'm having a stationary bicycle put in your room. A physical therapist will work with you and design a program of exercise just for your needs." Dr. Jacoby smiled. "I can tell that pleases you."

Katie nodded. "I'd like that a lot. I need to test this heart you've given me. And I've got some money to spend," she added, thinking of the Wish funds sitting in the bank.

"You can do it all, Katie," the doctor told her with a grin. "You just can't do it all at once."

She shot him a sideways glance. "We'll see," she muttered stubbornly under her breath.

Nine

"I WISH ALL my patients were as cooperative as you, Katie," Barry, the physical therapist, said with a grin. "Mostly, I get fifty-year-old men who've never done anything more physical than use the remote control on their TV set. They aren't the least bit interested in exercise."

"I am," Katie declared with determination. Actually, every muscle in her legs was protesting the workout on the stationary bicycle, but she knew from her athletic experience that the kind of pain she was feeling was good pain. "I haven't exercised like this since last spring, before I got sick," she told Barry. "It feels pretty good to sweat."

He laughed. "Don't overdo it, or the doc will have my hide. Now, stop and take your pulse. Tell me what you feel."

She quit pedaling and put her fingertips against her wrist and counted. The coursing of the blood through her veins sent out a steady rhythm, making her smile. She felt the heart—*her* heart— pounding in her chest, young and vibrant with health. It was a good heart, with a lifetime of work left in it.

At the end of sixty seconds, she told Barry her pulse rate. He flashed a wide smile. "That's good, Katie. Real good. You've been doing better every day this week."

"Tell that to my mom. If she had her way, I'd be an invalid for the rest of my life."

"She's scared," Barry said. "I see that kind of reaction in patients and their families all the time."

"Well, I'm not scared."

"You need a balance," Barry cautioned. "You can't abuse your new heart, either."

"All I want is for it to help me run again."

"Doc Jacoby told me you were once a track star."

"I plan to be one again," Katie replied with a lift of her chin. "Are you going to try and talk me out of it?"

"Not me. Transplant patients can do anything they want, so long as they take good care of themselves."

"We can?" This was the first positive word Katie had heard since her operation. "Tell me more."

"I've read about recipients becoming marathon runners. It takes a great deal of work and medical supervision, but it's possible."

Katie felt as if a door she'd been banging on for

months had suddenly swung open. "That's what I want to do—run. I used to be good at it, you know."

"You can test yourself in the Olympics," Barry said.

"The Olympics? I don't know if I'm *that* good."

Barry laughed. "The Transplant Olympics, I mean."

Katie eyed him skeptically. "Are you making fun of me?"

"No way. Years ago, when transplanting first started, most people died early on. In the mid-seventies, medicine almost gave up the operations altogether. The doctors knew how to do the surgeries, but the rejection problem couldn't be licked."

Katie squirmed. She'd come to fear the word *rejection* more than any other. "I thought the problem was under control."

"It's become less of a problem with cyclo-sporine."

"That's one of my medicines."

"You know what it is?"

Katie didn't have a clue. "A test-tube drug?"

Barry launched into a story. "Some microbiologist discovered it in a soil sample he'd dug up on a plateau in Norway when he was on vacation. He was searching for a new antibiotic, you know, like penicillin—and just happened on this new organic compound no one had ever seen before."

"You're making this up," Katie chided.

"It's the truth, Katie. The stuff wasn't worth a thing as an antibiotic, but another scientist noticed that in his laboratory, this compound had a powerful effect on the immune system. After a lot of testing, cyclosporine proved far better than steroids for handling rejection. Once that breakthrough came"—Barry shrugged—"transplants got popular again. And now more people are living than dying from them. So . . . the survivors get together once a year and have this big Olympics called the Transplant Games. They compete in athletic events, meet others like themselves, and put out the good word about organ donation."

"Where are these games held?"

"This year, they're in Los Angeles, on the UCLA campus. I've read that officials are expecting maybe six hundred participants."

"Six hundred and one," Katie said. Her pulse was tripping, but not from physical exertion.

Barry laughed and patted her shoulder. "They're held in July, Katie. You have a long way to go before you're competitive again."

"I'm willing to work hard."

Barry's brow puckered. "You'll just have to see how you're doing with your new heart. Remember, people hold the Games in order to bring national attention to the need for organ donation."

"Then, I'll be a walking billboard," Katie insisted. "Can you get more information about the Games for me?"

"Sure."

"Good." Katie put her feet back on the pedals of the stationary bike. "Let's get back to work."

"Now, Katie—"

"Oh, don't be a drag, Barry. I have enough problems with my parents—although Mom's worse than Dad."

That night, when she told her parents, each reacted just as Katie had predicted. Her dad perked up with interest. Her mother recoiled in fear. "I just don't think this therapist has any right to give you any false hopes," her mother said.

"Barbara, don't be so negative," Katie's dad said.

She shot him a scathing look. "I only want what's best for Katie."

"I have money enough to take us all," Katie declared. "You said I could spend my Wish money on something I really wanted. Well, I want this in the worst way."

"I think you should think about something else. You could buy a car for yourself," her mother suggested.

"You mean you'll let her drive?" her dad asked sarcastically. "Or does she need to get a personal chauffeur?"

"Really, Dan! I'm only thinking about Katie's overall safety."

Katie didn't feel like listening to them argue. In fact, she wasn't feeling well at all. Her head hurt, her hands and feet felt icy cold, and her body was weak and trembling. Perhaps she'd exercised too hard that afternoon, she told herself. "Could you not talk so loud?" Katie asked. "I have a headache."

Both her parents looked at her. Her mother's eyes narrowed. "Are you all right?" She placed her hand on Katie's forehead. "Dan, she's got a fever. Get a nurse."

"I'm fine, Mom," Katie mumbled, knowing that she wasn't.

In minutes, her room filled with nurses and technicians. Katie heard one nurse tell another, "Call Dr. Jacoby. Stat."

Katie tried to insist she was all right, but she couldn't make her mouth shape the words. Her parents huddled to one side, looking frightened. She struggled to tell them not to worry, that she would be fine.

When Dr. Jacoby came, he smoothed her brow and checked the results of her blood work on her medical chart. "We're moving you back into isolation, Katie."

"No . . ." she mumbled weakly. "I want to stay here."

"You can't. You're having an episode of rejection. You know that we've expected this."

"Please . . . make it go away." Tears slid from the corners of her eyes.

"We're working on it," Dr. Jacoby said. His expression was grim.

Katie cried as they began to roll her bed down the hall toward the ICU.

Josh made it a point of learning who Katie O'Roark's friends were at school. He learned that her best friend was a junior named Melody and that Melody enjoyed giving out frequent bulletins about Katie's health. As unobtrusively as possible, he hung on the fringes of the small groups that gathered whenever Melody gave an update. That was how he learned that Katie was undergoing rejection of her new heart and that she'd been moved into Intensive Care.

Josh could hardly handle the sense of despair that swept over him. *She can't die!* he told himself. She was his only link to Aaron. Katie had to live, because if she was alive, then a part of Aaron would be alive, too.

That night, he lay on his bed, listening to music and bouncing a basketball off the wall. The repetitious movement gave him something to focus on, something to anchor his sanity. Gramps came into the room after knocking and eyed Josh speculatively. "Your school called today," he said. "The office said you missed two days of classes. You leave here every morning, but you aren't going to school. Where are you going?"

Josh didn't know how to answer. He didn't want to upset his grandfather, but how could he explain that he went and sat in his car in the hospital parking lot, staring up at the ninth floor? "No place," he answered.

Gramps sat down on the bed. "I know you're still grieving for Aaron, boy. We both are. It's not something you can get over right away. Grieving's good—it's natural, and you can't put a time limit on it. What's not good is getting stuck in one part of it."

Josh nodded, not wanting to get into a discussion. He wanted to be left alone. "I wish I could

change what's happened." The sense of helpless-
ness he felt was overwhelming. He had no control
over Aaron's dying, no control over Katie's rejection. He didn't even know her, but he felt linked to
her.

"When you can't change things, you find a way
to live with them as they are. You find a way to
make peace with God and go on in spite of it."

Josh didn't think it was possible for him to overcome what was happening.

"That's what Aaron did," Gramps added.

"How?"

"When he knew it was impossible for him and
you to live at home anymore, he figured out a way
around it."

"We came here," Josh said.

"That's right. So, I'm asking you, if you can't
bring Aaron back from the grave, what can you do
to make your peace with his dying?"

The answer came to Josh in a flash of inspira-
tion. He could touch Katie O'Roark before she
died. Not in a secondhand way, as he'd been doing
so far, but in the flesh, with his own hands. By
touching her, he could connect with Aaron. He
twirled the basketball in his hands. "I'll think
about it," he told Gramps.

The old man rose and shuffled to the door. "The
Good Book says that by helping others, we help
ourselves. Josh, having you here with me is good
help. I wish I could offer you the same kind of
help. If you ever want to talk . . ."

The old man's eloquence reached inside Josh, making him soften, calming his fears. "You're good help to me, Gramps. Tonight, you've helped me a lot." The moment Gramps left, Josh began to formulate a plan.

Ten

JOSH BLENDED INTO the group of people as they stepped into the hospital elevator on the ground floor. He licked his lips, dry from inner tension. *Act as though you belong here,* he told himself. Only people who look nervous and out of place get noticed.

The elevator stopped on each floor. The door slid open, and visitors stepped out. Soon, Josh was the only occupant of the car, and he was startled when the door opened onto the ninth floor. The halls looked eerily empty as he exited. He stood still for a moment, to get his bearings and to calm his racing heart.

Deep breaths, he commanded silently. *Look as though you belong.* His brother had taught him the lesson years earlier, when Aaron had been fourteen and Josh only ten. Their mother had been in the hospital, put there by a pounding from their father's fists. Josh had cried for days, convinced that he wouldn't see his mother alive ever again.

"You want to see her?" Aaron asked.

"I can't go up there," Josh said, sniffing. Aaron was old enough to visit on patient floors; he wasn't.

"Sure you can. Just come up with me. Keep your eyes straight ahead, and look as if you belong. That way, no one will even notice you."

Josh had done exactly as he'd been told. He'd seen his mother, her face bandaged, her arm in a cast. She'd wept, and he'd clung to her as if she might disappear. Josh shook his head to clear out the long-ago memories of that other day in a hospital. If only Aaron were here with him now to help give him courage.

"Are you lost?"

The nurse's voice caused Josh to jump a foot. "Um—I was looking for the ICU," he said.

"It's at the end of the hall." She pointed. "Do you have a family member there? Only immediate family can be admitted to the unit, and then for only ten minutes at a visit. There's an ICU waiting room next door if you want to visit with someone's family."

"I'm not here to see anyone in particular," he replied, moistening his lips again. "You see, I'm doing a special report on intensive care for a science project. So, I'm up here sort of snooping around for information." Josh smiled, inwardly startled by the glib way the lie had flowed out of his mouth.

The nurse was young and pretty. She returned his smile. "I've only been here a week myself. I'm in training. I don't know much, but what I do know I'll be glad to tell you. I've had to do reports for classroom projects. Sometimes the books make everything so dull."

"Then you understand." Josh felt a wave of relief. "I'd really appreciate a guided tour."

"I can take you inside the unit, but not into any one patient's cubicle."

"Inside would be fine." He tagged along behind her, crossing his fingers in the hope that he could maintain his charade. She inserted a special card in a doorway security system. When the buzzer sounded, she led him into a large room that was lined with glass-enclosed cubicles. A central island allowed two nurses to see into every cubicle, as well as monitor banks of electronic equipment on one side of the room.

He listened as the nurse, Maria, explained to the other nurses what she was doing. He grinned at them innocently and rocked back on his heels, hoping the quaking of his insides didn't show on his face. The others seemed busy, distracted, so Maria launched into a spiel about the ICU while Josh pretended to be interested.

All the time, his gaze darted about. He knew that Katie lay in one of the cubicles. "Can I look inside the glass windows?" he asked when Maria paused for a breath. "I promise not to disturb anybody."

Maria looked hesitant, but finally said, "I guess so."

He walked slowly down one side of the room. In one cubicle lay a man hooked to machines. Another was empty. A third had a sign posted on the door that read: DO NOT ENTER. ISOLATION PROTOCOL. On the bed lay a girl. His breath jammed in his lungs. He knew he'd found Katie O'Roark. He stood at the glass partition, transfixed. Her dark hair spilled out onto the pillow, and she looked frail and impossibly thin. Her bed was surrounded by machines, wires, tubes, and lines.

Without realizing it, Josh had pressed so close to the glass that his nose was touching it. His heart hammered against his ribs. His fingers curled on the glass. *Katie. Aaron.* Both only a few feet away.

"You're not really doing a report on the ICU, are you?"

Maria's question caused cold sweat to break out on Josh's face. He glanced sideways at her. "I'm sorry I lied." His words came haltingly. "But I had to see her. Please don't be angry at me. Don't call the cops. I'll leave."

The nurse touched his arm. "She's your girlfriend, isn't she?"

Josh felt as if he'd been given a reprieve. "How did you guess?" he asked. Another lie.

"It's written all over your face that she's special to you. Don't panic. I'm not going to throw you out. Take a minute and look at her. Don't let the others know, okay?" She gestured toward the nurse's station.

"It's our secret ... and thanks." Josh continued to stare at Katie. He longed to touch her. He supposed he was going nuts. What else but insanity could have driven him to haunt a hospital for weeks, hang around the lobby, sneak up to the ICU, and lie to get inside so that he could gaze longingly at a girl he didn't know and had never met? "How is she doing?"

"Actually, pretty well."

Josh glanced quickly at Maria, then back at Katie. "She is?" His breath made a foggy place on the window.

"With the machines and all, I know it's pretty intimidating, but she turned a corner this morning. Dr. Jacoby thinks he's got her episode of rejection under control."

Josh's knees went weak. "That's good."

"Maybe they'll move her back into her room in a few days. I know her parents will be relieved. They've been here day and night."

Josh couldn't tear his eyes away from Katie. He saw her chest rising and falling. The image soothed him. Aaron's heart was keeping her alive. He watched as Katie's head turned on the pillow. He held his breath as he saw her eyes struggle open, focus, and stare directly into his. Josh gasped and jumped backward. "I should be going," he mumbled. For some reason, he felt revealed and naked.

A puzzled frown creased Maria's forehead. "Maybe you should."

Josh walked quickly to the door and out into the corridor. "Thanks," he called over his shoulder to the young nurse pursuing him. "I really appreciate your letting me in." He punched the elevator button. When it didn't arrive promptly, he ducked through the stairwell exit.

"Wait!" he heard the nurse call.

"See you next time!" Josh yelled. His voice reverberated in the hollow stairwell as he hurried downward. He chased its echo all the way to the ground floor.

Katie drifted, feeling as if she were again floating on a warm sea. She was more aware this time. She heard voices, recognizing her mother's and father's whispers. She wanted to tell them, "I'm fine. I'll be fine," but couldn't.

She had glimpses of people coming in and out, of bending and probing. All she could see of them were their eyes sandwiched between green paper masks and green paper head coverings. Didn't they know she wanted to see their lips and cheeks and chins? Didn't anyone realize what it was like to be handled through the barrier of latex gloves?

She felt like some laboratory rat in a glass cage, trapped on a bed, held in place by wires and tubes. She wanted out. She wanted to go home. She wanted to feel the sunlight on her skin once more.

Katie knew she'd lost all the progress she'd gained in working out on the stationary bike. She'd have to start all over again. *Hold on, heart,* she said to herself over and over. She thought about JWC, who knew what it was like to lie in a hospital ". . . feeling lonely and scared." Maybe when JWC heard about Katie, he or she would come and talk to her. It would be nice to talk to someone her age again.

Katie struggled to open her eyes. The longing to be with someone like herself was tangible. When her eyes opened, she was looking through the glass wall of her cubicle. A boy with red hair was standing there, looking in at her. It was as if her longing had melded with her imagination and conjured him up from thin air. Katie was so startled that she didn't even blink.

All at once, the boy vanished. She tried to call him back, but her voice wouldn't work. Moments later, her eyelids closed as sleep reached out for her. He had simply been a figment of her imagination. Disappointment crowded in on her. He'd been an illusion, a fantasy, constructed out of her loneliness to fill a need for *someone* human to touch her.

Eleven

KATIE BREATHED A deep, contented sigh. Even though she was only allowed to sit in a wheelchair in the visitation room, her sense of freedom and mobility felt incredible. She'd been returned to her room from the ICU two days before and allowed to leave her room for the first time that morning. With a nurse's help, she'd washed her hair, put on makeup, and dressed in the beautiful royal blue velvety bathrobe her parents had bought her.

After lunch, she'd worked with Barry and the stationary bike. After she'd told him she was going "stir crazy," he'd helped her into the wheelchair and she'd rolled herself down the hall under the watchful eyes of the nurses. Katie rolled over to the window and peered out. The weather was sunny, but she could tell it was cold. The trees were barren, and the ground looked brown and lifeless. Typical of November.

"I've been here forever," she muttered under her breath, recalling the glorious autumn she'd left behind when she'd entered the hospital. She still couldn't pin Dr. Jacoby down on a release date.

"Soon," was all he'd say.

Soon. The word had lost its meaning. Katie tried not to be glum, but now that she was feeling better, the days seemed impossibly long. At least, she could have visitors—Melody had been the first. She'd come the night before and cried the whole time she visited.

"I can't believe you're actually all right," Melody had said between sobs. "I never thought I was going to see you again. First you were sick, then dying, then the operation . . . and now . . . now you're alive and *beautiful.* Oh, Katie, it's a miracle!"

Katie felt that while it certainly might appear miraculous to Melody, only she knew how complicated her "miracle" had been. And how painful.

"I'll come visit you every day. I'll tell everyone at school how great you're doing," Melody insisted. "Everybody asks about you. In fact, the main office puts updates about you on the central bulletin board. I think Mr. Clausen is going to declare a Katie O'Roark Day when you come back to school."

Katie was mortified. She didn't want all the attention, especially since she hadn't done anything to deserve it. It wasn't like winning a race, or the medallion for top high school female runner in the district. So far, all she'd done was survive a heart transplant.

Katie sighed and pushed her wheelchair away from the window. She glanced around the room and saw that a few more patients had entered, some with visitors. The people in street clothes looked out of place to her. Actually, she felt a twinge of jealousy. She'd give anything to put on blue jeans and a sweatshirt again.

From the corner of her eye, she saw a boy with red hair who was about her age. He stood near the doorway, looking nervous. With a start, she realized he was watching her, because he kept diverting his gaze when she glanced his way. *Odd*, Katie told herself. Katie had a nagging sense she'd seen him before, even though she couldn't place him. As nonchalantly as possible, she rolled her wheelchair closer, picking up a magazine as she passed a table.

She flipped through the magazine, pretending to be interested, all the while glancing discreetly toward the boy. Even though he also picked up a magazine, Katie could tell that he was preoccupied with studying her. Suddenly, she grew self-conscious. Was something wrong with the way she looked? She'd thought she looked better than she had in months when she'd left her hospital room that afternoon. Why was he watching her?

A flash of insight caused her to gasp. Could he somehow be connected to the mysterious Wish Foundation? Katie turned the chair and in one smooth move rolled it right up to him, almost pinning him against the wall. "Excuse me," she said. "By any chance, are your initials JWC?"

She caught him totally off guard, and his face turned as red as his hair. "Yes," he stammered, trying to get out of her way. "I mean, no. That is, my first name begins with a J, but that's all."

Katie felt both disappointed and foolish. She thought that he was good-looking, tall and lanky with a square jaw and gold-flecked brown eyes. In an effort to appear in control, she asked, "What's the J for?"

"Um—Joshua," he said. "But everybody calls me Josh."

"Where do you go to school?"

"Ann Arbor High."

"So do I. When I'm not in the hospital." She tipped her head upward. "Do I know you from school?"

He flushed beet red once more. "No. I mean . . . I just transferred in September."

Why couldn't she shake the feeling that she'd seen him somewhere before? "Do you like it?"

"Sure. It's okay."

Katie was running out of small talk, yet she still couldn't place him. However, it was so good to be around someone her own age that she didn't want him to leave—even if he did look cornered. "Would you like to sit and talk to me? You don't have to," she added quickly. "It's just that I've been cooped up in this place for so long, I'm ready to scream." She tacked on an encouraging smile.

He dropped his gaze. "Well, maybe for a few minutes."

She rolled toward an empty sofa on the far side of the room where he sat and peered anxiously around. "Are you waiting for someone?" she asked. Secretly, she hoped not.

"No," he said.

"So, why are you here?" She watched him lace his fingers together and stare down at them. Once she asked, it occurred to Katie that it did seem strange that he would be here for no reason. "I guess you probably thought I was crazy asking you about your initials," she said.

"Why did you?"

"Someone with those initials has been very nice to me, but I've never met the person. Are you sure you're not JWC?"

"My name's Josh Martel." He jerked his head up and looked at her hard, almost as if he expected her to recognize the name.

Katie searched her memory, but drew a blank. "I guess I don't know you," she admitted haltingly. "I can't help it, though . . . you really look familiar to me."

He suddenly appeared more at ease. "I have a 'regular' face. Nothing special."

"It's probably all the medications I'm taking. I'll bet they've turned my brain into soup," Katie remarked wryly. "I can't wait to get out of this place."

"How much longer will you be here?"

"Who knows? Until my doctor thinks my heart's fit to travel."

"You have a bad heart?" Josh's expression looked concerned.

"The doctor's fixed it," Katie said, deciding that her story was much too long and involved to tell. Besides, she didn't want Josh to think of her as an invalid. "I'll probably be running foot races by this summer."

"Are you coming back to school soon?"

"I don't know. I have to recuperate at home first, but eventually I'll come back. What class are you in?"

"I'm a junior."

Katie smiled brightly. "Hey—same as me."

"I know—I mean—you look like a junior." Josh's face flushed red.

Katie's eyes narrowed, and she studied him more closely. He seemed acutely embarrassed, almost guilty, as if he'd been caught doing something wrong. All at once, everything clicked into place. She remembered opening her eyes in the ICU and seeing a red-haired boy with the same expression of embarrassed guilt staring at her through the glass wall. "You were the guy in the ICU!" she blurted out.

Josh almost leapt up, but Katie's hand reached out and stopped him. "Don't go," she said. "I didn't mean to scare you off." Now she was embarrassed. He probably thought she had lost her mind.

He didn't pull away from her, only glanced down at her hand on his arm. "I was the guy in Intensive Care," he admitted.

"I thought I had imagined you," Katie said softly. "You were real." Josh nodded. "But why? Why were you there? Why were you looking at me?"

Josh's cheeks colored. "You probably think I'm weird."

Until he said it, the idea hadn't crossed Katie's mind. "Forget weird—but I am curious."

Josh released a long, pent-up sigh. "I wanted to see the person who had received my brother's heart."

Katie felt as if all the air had gone from the room and time was standing still. "Your brother?"

"You see, he died, and my Gramps and I okayed donating his organs. No one knew . . . no one knows. I put it all together when I read your father's column about his daughter, Katie, who'd gotten a second chance at life with a heart transplant. There were some other details in the story . . . and with the timing of Aaron's—" He interrupted himself. "Well . . . I figured it out." Josh was inches from her face.

"I wanted to see you," he explained. "Somehow, knowing that Aaron's heart was alive inside you made him alive again for me." He glanced away, looking self-conscious and a little scared. "I can't explain it really. I'm sorry if I've pestered you."

For a moment, Katie couldn't speak. The whole scenario seemed unreal. Then, a mist of tears came to her eyes and a thick lump closed off her throat. "Thank you," she whispered.

Josh looked up quickly. "I won't bother you anymore." He moved, as if to rise and leave.

"Wait a minute. Don't go." She fumbled with the pocket of her bathrobe and withdrew a stethoscope. He looked so surprised that she laughed. "I know . . . most girls carry a brush. I have to do this several times a day, so I drag it everywhere."

"Do what?"

"This." Katie leaned forward and placed the earpieces of the stethoscope gently into Josh's ears. She took the other end and placed it under her robe, snugly against the warm flesh near her left breast. "Listen," she urged, never taking her eyes from Josh's face.

She watched his expression go from wariness to surprise to wonderment. She saw his golden brown eyes fill with tears and his lashes sweep downward as his eyes closed. She knew what he was hearing— the faint *whoosh-whoosh* of her healthy, beating heart. She heard him exhale and felt the pepperminty warmth of his breath on her cheek as he whispered, "Hey, bro."

Twelve

JOSH COULD HARDLY swallow around the knot that blocked his throat as he listened to the steady rhythm of Aaron's heart. How wonderful it sounded! How strong and sturdy. For an instant, he felt suspended in time and space, caught between the present and the past. Aaron was truly alive in the body of Katie O'Roark. Overwhelmed, he felt a tear escape and trickle down his cheek. His eyes flew open when he felt Katie's finger brush it tenderly.

Josh straightened. Unashamed, he gazed straight at her and saw that her own tears were wetting her cheeks. She dropped the end of the stethoscope and gently held his face between her palms. "Thank you, Josh Martel. Because of you . . . because of Aaron . . . I'm alive. I was almost dead, you know, when Aaron's heart became available. Without it, I'd be in a grave right now. I've wondered so much about my donor. I prayed that I could one day meet the family. Did you know that?"

"No."

"It's true. My parents and I—we're all so very, very grateful to you. I've wanted to know about my donor, but the hospital tells you so little. They act as if they want to keep it a secret, as if recipients shouldn't know who their donor is. I wanted to know more than anything. Will you tell me about Aaron?"

Josh's emotions churned, jumbled and wild. He had slipped into the hospital that afternoon only to catch another glimpse of Katie. He couldn't help himself. He was drawn to her like a moth to a flame. When she'd struck up a conversation with him, he'd lost control of his role as an observer. At first, he couldn't believe she hadn't recognized him from the ICU, but when it became evident that she hadn't, he'd allowed himself to be questioned by her.

When he'd given his name and she hadn't responded to it, he'd realized that she honestly didn't know how they were linked. When she'd reached over and touched him, it was as if they'd connected spiritually as well as physically. And then, when she'd let him listen to Aaron's heart . . .

"I would like to tell you about my brother . . . just not right now," he said, clearing his throat.

"But you will tell me? You will come back?"

Josh knew there was no way on earth he could
stay away. Not telling her about Aaron was tearing
him up inside. He *had* to share his memories, and
his feelings, with someone. "I'll be back."

"I know my mom and dad will want to meet
you. Is that okay? I promise that my dad won't do
a column about you."

Her joke made him smile. "I'd like to meet
them," he told her. He rose to leave. She took his
hand, as if uncertain whether or not to let him go.
The gesture touched him. "Can I come to your
room next time? Or should I run the risk of 'acci-
dentally' bumping into you in the visitors' room?"
he asked.

He watched her smile and decided she was beautiful. "My room is fine. Maybe I could meet your
grandfather, too."

"Once I tell him about you, I'm sure he'll want
to meet you." Josh squeezed her hand. "One question before I go—who's this JWC you asked me
about?"

Katie shrugged. "As I told you, I don't really
know, but he or she's been good to me. I'll tell you
all about it sometime."

"Funny how we have the same first initial," Josh
said.

"A coincidence," Katie replied. "You look perfectly healthy, while JWC has health problems.
That much I know."

Josh peered down into her upturned face and for
a moment had the bizarre urge to take her with
him. He didn't want to leave her, yet she looked

tired and fragile, and he didn't want her to have a relapse. "I'll see you soon," he promised, then turned and fairly coasted out the door.

"You actually met him?" Her father sounded incredulous.

"All because of your column," Katie said. "But *please* don't write another one about me." She was propped up in bed, and her parents had come for their evening visit.

"I'm not sure how I feel about this," her mother said. "I don't think recipients should meet a donor's family."

Katie felt exasperated. "What's he going to do, Mom? Take the heart back?"

Her mother flushed. "It may be too much emotional stress on you. On them, too. Did he mention his parents? Think how they must be feeling. I know what it feels like to watch someone you love lie dying."

"Josh only mentioned his grandfather. I didn't ask about his and Aaron's parents." The oddity of it suddenly struck Katie. Where were Josh's parents? Why had only he and Gramps made the decision to donate Aaron's organs?

"Well, I'd like to meet this young man," Katie's dad said. "I'd like to shake his hand and tell him thanks. A lot more people could be saved if more people were willing to donate their organs. Maybe I'll do a column about it."

"Daddy—"

"Not about you. About organ donation."

"I don't want the whole world to know," Katie said. "Unless Josh does. I think we should protect his privacy."

"That's fine with us," her dad agreed. "However you want to handle it."

Josh and Gramps came the next evening, and after a round of introductions, the elderly man shuffled closer to Katie's bed. "You're right, Josh, she's a pretty girl."

Katie felt self-conscious, and Josh didn't look too comfortable, either. "I look better now that they've cut back on my steroid dose. For a while, I resembled a Halloween pumpkin," she said.

"I can't imagine that you ever looked bad," Gramps said. He turned toward Katie's parents. "Aaron would be pleased to know Katie's alive because of his heart. He was an athlete, you know."

"I didn't know," Katie's father replied, his face bright with interest.

Katie was surprised, too, but delighted. She'd received an athlete's heart, which put her that much closer to her dream of running again.

Gramps glanced at Josh, who explained, "Aaron was the University of Michigan football kicker who died on the field in the first game of the season."

Katie's dad looked stunned. "Aaron Martel? Of course! I remember when it happened, but I was so caught up in Katie at the time that I never reported on it. One of my colleagues did. Then, that night, when the call came that they'd found Katie a heart—well, I didn't have time to follow up on the story." Mr. O'Roark shook his head. "It was a real tragedy, and we're sorry. He was a fine football player. I remember his stats from preseason."

Katie noticed that Josh had turned his head as a look of pain crossed his face. She felt unbearable pity for him and wished there were something she could do to help him.

"Josh here is an athlete, too," Gramps said, in an attempt to smooth over the awkward moment.

"Track," Josh said quickly. "Aaron was into football, and I took up track.,"

Katie sat upright. "Me, too!" she cried.

"I know." Josh's honey-color eyes bore into her. "I read it in your dad's column."

The mention of the column brought comic relief, and all of them laughed. "What can I say? I love having a jock for a daughter," Katie's dad kidded.

Gramps took Katie's hand in his. "You take good care of Aaron's heart, young lady. And when you run your first race, I'll be cheering for you."

"I'm not sure Katie will be resuming her track career," Katie's mom said. "Her doctors must approve any exertion, any strenuous exercise."

Katie bit her tongue, not wanting to have a scene in front of strangers. "We'll see," she said stubbornly. "The quality of my life was supposed to improve with the transplant."

"It has improved. You're alive," her mother countered.

Gramps turned toward his grandson. "It's getting late. Maybe we'd better get home."

Josh agreed, and Katie watched them leave after

extracting a promise from Josh that he'd come again the next day. "We have a lot to talk about," she called to him.

Once they were gone, Katie's mother said, "We'd better go, too. I promised one of the schools I'd substitute-teach tomorrow. Can I get you anything?" She acted casual, as if her and Katie's exchange about exercise hadn't occurred.

Katie sank down into the bed. "All I want is to get out of here."

"In due time," her mother assured her. "But let's not push it."

Katie felt like screaming. Couldn't anyone understand that she was fine now—that because of Aaron's healthy heart, a great surgeon, and the wonder drug cyclosporine, she was well? She wanted out. She wanted to pick up her life again. She wanted her freedom. She had been given a second chance at life—if anyone would allow her to take it!

Thirteen

"How often do I have to have this done?" Katie asked Dr. Jacoby.

"After this heart biopsy, you'll have another at three months and another at six months. Eventually, you'll have one a year," Dr. Jacoby explained as a nurse readied instruments in the procedure room. "If today's test looks good, I'll release you."

Katie lay on a stretcher while the doctor cleaned her neck with an iodine solution. The promise of going home made it difficult for her to lie still for the procedure. "Why do I have to have heart biopsies?"

"They reveal whether or not your body has accepted your new heart."

"I thought it had."

"This is the only way to know for certain. Now,

relax. I'm pretty good at this procedure, if I do say so myself."

Relax! What a joke, Katie thought. How was she supposed to relax when a doctor was about to make an incision in her neck, thread a special wire along her jugular vein and into her heart, and snip off a piece to be examined under a microscope? "Will it hurt?"

"Done properly, it shouldn't. I've deadened the skin at the site of the incision, and you have no nerve endings inside your veins. Do you want your parents in here with you?"

"Are you serious? Dad almost passes out when he watches the lab draw blood, and Mom acts as if I'm going to break apart."

Dr. Jacoby smiled. "They're just concerned, and their behavior is very typical. You want to watch this on the fluoroscope?" He motioned to a portable X-ray camera with a screen for following the path of the biopsy instrument.

"Can I?"

"You'll be getting a lot of biopsies over the years. You may as well see what's being done."

She was nervous, but became curious after the sting of the injection administering the local anesthetic was over. "Will I have a scar on my neck?"

"A small one."

"Will I have a new scar after each biopsy?"

"Yes."

"That stinks. I'll look like Dracula's girlfriend."

Dr. Jacoby laughed. "Katie, I don't think I've ever had a patient with your sense of humor."

Katie watched the procedure on the TV screen as objectively as possible, trying not to think of what she was seeing as *her* insides. The wirelike instrument with pincers on the end slid along her neck and into the chamber of her heart. *Aaron's heart.* She'd give Josh visitation rights. *What an odd way to meet a guy.* The idea caused her to smile faintly.

"The human heart," Dr. Jacoby said as he worked. "It beats one hundred thousand times a day, pumping two thousand gallons of blood for eighty—sometimes ninety years and more. I can't believe we'll ever come up with a mechanical pump that can perform as well."

"This is a good heart, isn't it?"

"Very good."

"Barry says I'm doing well in my exercise program."

"I know."

"He told me about the Transplant Games. I want to run in them." What she had wanted to say was, *I'm going to run in the Transplant Games.*

Dr. Jacoby caught her eye, then resumed his work. "Katie, I'm not going to say you *can't* do anything. I *am* going to warn you, though, that no matter how good you feel, you've still got medical problems. Frankly, compared with most patients in the transplant program, you received your transplant very quickly. I have patients who've been waiting for years; others have died waiting for a suitable organ. The waiting process often makes people more aware of what an extraordinary blessing a donor organ can be."

"Don't you think I'm grateful? I am. But I don't want to always be afraid to live, either. Don't you see? I can be a real asset for organ donation. I can be an advocate. If I do well—really well—on the track, thousands of people will know. They'll be able to see that donating organs is a good thing and that recipients can live normal, useful lives. Who wants to be an invalid? When people see someone with a transplant doing well, they'll be doubly impressed."

"Perhaps we should send you on a PR tour. You make a good case," Dr. Jacoby said as he stitched up the small incision. "Look, continue to work with Barry. He'll outline a gradual program to get you back in shape. Personally, I would like to see you aim for next year's Games. I know that's hard because you feel good now."

"Better than I have in almost a year," Katie admitted.

"Nevertheless, when I do send you home, I'll want you to stay housebound with light exercise for around six to nine weeks. Then, after regular checkups and another biopsy, if all's well, you can return to school."

"That won't be until at least January, though," Katie said, dismayed.

"Correct. And the Games are in July. That's really not a lot of time to be fully competitive." Dr. Jacoby gave her a sidelong glance. "Of course, I'm assuming you're planning on running to win, not just running for fun, which is another conversation altogether."

"That's the only way I've ever run," Katie said.

"I'm not surprised."

"But you're not telling me that I can't be competitive by July, are you?"

Dr. Jacoby slapped the palm of his hand against his forehead. "You're as stubborn as a bulldog, Katie O'Roark."

She offered him a dazzling grin. "That's true, but how else can a person become a winner unless she sets her sights on being one?"

"Talk to Barry," Dr. Jacoby said, signaling the nurse that Katie could be taken back to her room. "And follow what he tells you, to the letter."

The biopsy showed that Katie's body was accepting Aaron's heart, and Dr. Jacoby told her, "Pack your things. I'm tossing you out of here."

As Katie left the hospital, the whole transplant team, the nurses on the ninth floor, and every member of the staff who'd worked with her lined the hallway and applauded. She sat in the wheelchair in jeans and a sweater, holding a bouquet of roses, her parents on either side of her. As she rolled toward the elevator, watching their faces, seeing their smiles, hearing their good wishes for her, she cried.

At the elevator, Dr. Jacoby pushed the button for the lobby. "Are they clapping because they're glad to be rid of me?" she quipped to the doctor.

He laughed. "That's right. They never want to see you up here again—unless it's for a friendly visit."

Barry offered up the Vulcan peace sign, " 'Live

long and prosper,' " he said. "You call me if you need anything."

She had lists of information and fistfuls of pills going home with her. At the lobby door, looking outside into the cold November morning, she experienced a twinge of panic. Here in the hospital, she was surrounded by people who could help her at a moment's notice. At home, she'd be depending on her parents and herself. The idea was scary. She didn't want to be dependent on her parents. She'd spent sixteen years learning how to be independent of them. What if something came up none of them could handle?

Katie could tell by the pinched expression on her mother's face that she, too, was feeling the strain. When her mom helped Katie into the car, Katie felt the icy coldness of her hands and realized that her mother was probably panic-stricken. All of them had a lot of unwanted responsibility thrust upon them because of her transplant. She told herself that if she was ever going to break free again, she'd have to be the strong one and act unafraid. "Come on, Mom," Katie joked playfully. "We can do this. You know what they say—this is the first day of the rest of my life."

Her mother gave her a wan smile, took hold of her hand, and didn't let go all the way home.

Fourteen

❦

"I CAN'T FIGURE out how you pulled this off, Katie," Melody exclaimed.

"Pulled what off?" Katie asked. She'd been home for weeks, spending mornings with a tutor to catch up on her schoolwork, and afternoons with her friends whenever they dropped by after school. She and Melody were playing a halfhearted game of Scrabble one cold, rainy Friday afternoon.

"You spend weeks and weeks in the hospital in virtual isolation, and you still manage to meet Josh Martel—one of the cutest guys at school. How did you do that?" Melody slouched in her chair across from Katie, grumbling.

Katie smiled sweetly. "I told you, he wandered into the visitors' lounge at the hospital, and I was desperate for human contact. So, I pinned him against a wall with my wheelchair and told him if he didn't promise to come see me every day, I'd break both his legs."

Melody rolled her eyes in exasperation. "Maybe I should check in to the hospital. I haven't had a single meaningful date this year." She fiddled with several of the game tiles. "I remember seeing him in the halls at school. He always keeps to himself, though—kind of a loner, you know."

Katie knew. Josh came to her house often, but he rarely talked about himself. "I'm sure he just feels sorry for me," Katie said. "And besides, how many girls does he know who've had their hearts replaced?"

"Are you saying that he's hanging around for the sake of bragging rights? Get real, Katie! He likes you. I can tell."

Katie wanted to believe Melody. She was half sorry she couldn't tell her friend the whole truth, but she had sworn to protect Josh's privacy about the origin of her heart. Deep down, she knew that some of Josh's attraction to her was *because* of Aaron's heart. Not that Josh was obsessed or anything, but it was obvious to her how much he'd loved his brother. And how much he missed him.

She thought back to the first time he'd come over, bringing photographs of Aaron. The moment she glimpsed at Aaron's face smiling up at her, Katie started crying and couldn't stop.

"What's wrong? Are you all right?" Josh asked.

She was crying so hard, she could only nod in an attempt to assure him she was fine and to eliminate the worried expression on his face. She thought that the two brothers looked very much alike, except Aaron's hair was brown and his eyes were hazel. Katie stared for a long time at the photo of him wearing a graduation cap and gown. Finally, she blew her nose and said, "I'm sorry. I didn't mean to fall apart that way."

"I didn't mean to upset you. I thought you wanted to see my brother."

"You know I did. And it didn't upset me. It just made me so sad. As long as I never put a face with my donor, it was easier to accept the idea that a real human being had died and that I'd been given a part of him. Now, seeing him, knowing that he was real and seeing what he looked like . . . I can't explain it." She shook her head, wishing she could put into words what she was feeling.

"I understand," Josh said. "That's the way I felt about seeing you. It was something I had to do because it would bring Aaron back to me in a way. I couldn't tell anyone because I thought I'd be committed to the funny farm."

Katie touched his arm. "So, here we are, two strangers brought together by a guy who never had anything to say about it."

Josh nodded. "That's about it. I'm glad I know you, though. It helps."

For a long moment, neither of them said anything; they simply stared into each other's eyes. When she felt color begin to creep up her cheeks and her pulse quicken, she broke the eye contact and began rifling through the other pictures. "Is this one of him in his football uniform?" she asked. It was a dumb question, because it was obvious that Aaron was in uniform.

"High school," Josh said. "Gramps and I never got around to taking one of him in his college uniform. I just figured there'd be plenty of time to do it."

"My dad says you've got to do something the minute it crosses your mind, or the opportunity will get away from you."

"I like your dad," Josh said. "I like your whole family."

"They like you, too, Josh. Especially Daddy." She laughed. "All these years, I've had to be the son he always wanted. I tease him about it a lot."

"I can tell he wouldn't have it any other way."

She sorted through more of the photos. They all seemed to be of Aaron and Josh, none with either of their parents. She started to ask about it, but thought better of it. She didn't want to pry and felt that if he wanted to open up to her, he would do so when he felt the time was right. "Do you mind if I hang on to these for a while?" she asked.

Josh hesitated, and she quickly added, "I'll take good care of them, I swear."

He plucked one from the pile. "All right. Just let me take this one back home with me. I can't let them all go."

His sentiment touched her. There was a sadness about him that transcended the death of his brother. Katie didn't know how, but she sensed that Josh had been deeply wounded.

"He's a loner, all right," Katie heard Melody repeat. "I see him on the indoor track every morning for a workout. He doesn't say much to anyone, just runs his laps and goes off to classes."

The image of early morning workouts with the track team caused Katie to feel a sharp pang of regret. She should be working with the team, as she had in the past. She felt robbed, cheated. "I'm going to run again," she said.

Melody drew back, her eyes wide. "Are you serious? How can you?"

Katie felt a sudden quick rise of anger. "Good grief, I'm not handicapped," she said, knowing she was beginning to sound like a broken record. "Heart transplant patients can live regular lives, you know. Why, they even have special Olympic-style games for us."

"You're going to participate?" Melody sounded incredulous. "Your parents will let you?"

"I plan to go, no matter what they say." Katie lifted her chin. "And next year, I'll be back running track for the high school."

"What are you telling your friends?" Katie's dad wandered into the room on the tail end of their conversation. He came over to Katie, hugged her shoulders, and planted a kiss on top of her head.

One thing about her transplant, Katie thought wryly, her parents had become much more affectionate toward her. "I said, I'm going to take all-city in my senior year. Is that a problem for you?"

Her father looked as if he was going to say something negative, then shrugged and gave her a big smile. "Not for me. You know how I'd like to write another column about my girl."

"Oh, Daddy—"

Melody giggled. "What about me? Will you write about me, too, Mr. O'Roark?"

"If you earn some bodacious award, you bet." He went on to ask her several questions about the upcoming track season, and Katie could only listen. She felt left out and resented it. All she wanted was to be a part of it all again. She was tired of taking it easy. Sick and tired of playing by everybody else's rules while life passed her by.

That night, she took her prescribed pills and went to bed. She lay in the dark and traced the path of the scar from her neck to her stomach with the tips of her fingers. Her mother had been right, the scar *was* shrinking; but Katie knew it would never go away. It would always be there to remind her that she was living by the grace of a stranger's heart and the skill of a dedicated surgeon. Plus, the pills she took three times a day were a constant reminder that she owed her daily existence to a microbe as common as dirt. Of course, she was grateful. Who wouldn't be? It was just—*Just what?* she asked herself.

Her thoughts drifted to JWC, the one person who truly understood what learning to live with health problems was all about. The kinship Katie felt with this mysterious person was uncanny. No one knew what her life was like. Josh came the closest, but even he couldn't grasp what compromises she'd have to make in order to take advantage of the "new" life her transplant had afforded her.

Katie thought about the money. Didn't everyone dream of winning the lottery, or of hitting a jackpot? Yet, when it came right down to it, such a large amount of money as the Wish Foundation had given to her came with an equal amount of responsibility. It was difficult for her to dwell on spending it, especially on something that didn't benefit humanity in some grand way.

"I want to have some fun," Katie whispered to herself in the dark. She was tired of confinement, sick of rules about what she could and couldn't do. She longed for the days before her heart became diseased. In those days, she'd been able to do anything she wanted, physically. She'd been able to run like the wind . . . Confused, frustrated, Katie cried herself to sleep.

Sometime later, she awoke to the sound of voices coming from down the hall. Groggily, Katie sat upright. The voices were coming from her parents' room, and they sounded angry and loud.

Fifteen

THE SOUND OF their voices rose and fell, and occasionally Katie heard her name mentioned. Alarmed, she tossed off the covers and scooted out of her warm bed. Shivering, she wrapped her blue velvet robe around herself and eased down the hallway. The closer she got to her parents' room, the louder and more distinct their voices became.

". . . can't believe you'd encourage such lunacy, Dan!" Katie heard her mother shout.

"Lunacy! Because she wants to resume a normal life? What's crazy about that?" Katie heard her father shout back.

"A normal life, yes! She should have a normal life. But tell me, what's normal about her running in races that could possibly kill her?"

"Where do you get your medical information,

Barbara, *The Farmer's Almanac*? Running won't kill her! If anything, it can help prolong her life."

"Oh, give me a break!" Katie heard her mother slam a closet door, as if to punctuate her sentence. "Katie isn't your typical athlete anymore. She was hours away from dying, Dan, or have you forgotten what it was like before her transplant? She couldn't even shuffle across the floor without an oxygen mask."

"No, I haven't forgotten." Her father's voice sounded harsh. "I remember every moment of that living hell. I'd sit in my office, and every time the phone rang, my stomach would tie in knots. I was afraid it would be you, telling me she'd been taken to the hospital—or worse—that she was dead.

"Barb, don't you see? All that's behind her now." Her father's voice turned cajoling. "She has a brand-new lease on life, and she wants all the things that she had before that lousy virus attacked her heart. Katie's smart; she won't act foolish. She's a natural athlete. She knows how to train and how to pace herself."

"I can't believe what I'm hearing," Katie heard her mother answer, with an unmistakable hint of tears in her voice. "You would allow her to risk her life so that you can have your 'jock' daughter back, wouldn't you? It's eating at you that Katie isn't going to be your perfect little athletic wonder ever again."

"That's a low blow, Barb. And completely untrue. Is that what you honestly think? That all I'm interested in is her athletic prowess?"

"I think it's a factor," Katie's mother replied defiantly. "I think you miss her athletic status, the common ground the two of you shared."

Katie's heart hammered. She knew that she shouldn't be eavesdropping, yet she couldn't docilely head back down the hall, either. This argument between her parents might be setting the course of her life. She braced her hand on the wall, waiting for her father's comeback.

At last, she heard him say, "And what about you, Barb? How's it helping Katie to have you smothering her to death?"

"Smothering her! I love her. I'm scared for her. We almost lost her once. I won't go through that again just so she can run in a few track events, so that her father can write about her in his column."

"For crying out loud! Give me some credit for a little sense, will you! If Katie never runs another step, if she never goes away to college, if she lives with us for the rest of her life, it will be fine with me. I would lock her in her room before I'd allow her to do anything to harm herself in any way. All I've been trying to tell you is that she's determined to live as normal a life as possible. And for Katie, *normal* is running. As her parents, we're going to have to make some kind of peace with her medical condition and her willpower. If we don't, we risk alienating her completely."

"And if we do, she may die," Katie's mother countered.

Katie had heard enough. She stole quietly back to her room and slipped under the covers without taking off her robe. She huddled in a ball, trying to get warm, because she felt a chill that had little to do with the temperature of the air. She lay awake in the dark for a long time, pondering what she had overheard. It was obvious that her mother would never be persuaded that running wasn't going to harm her, and that while her father saw Katie's side more favorably, he probably wouldn't go against his wife's wishes. Nor, Katie told herself, would it be fair of her to divide them.

Katie shivered, feeling more depressed than ever. Suddenly, the words from her Wish letter floated into her memory. JWC had written, ". . . I can give you one wish, as someone did for me. My wish helped me find purpose, faith, and courage."

Katie knew that she already had a purpose. She also knew that she had faith in herself to accomplish her purpose. What she desperately needed was courage. She knew that the money alone wouldn't buy it, but taking her cue from the secretive JWC, Katie vowed to search for it—no matter what it cost her.

"I didn't believe it when Melody told me you were coming here all by yourself every morning," Josh said, falling in alongside Katie as she jogged around the indoor track.

"Don't set your workout pace by me," Katie told him breathlessly, hardly glancing over at him. "I'll only slow you down and throw you off your training schedule."

Josh's arm darted out and stopped her progress around the track.

"What are you doing?" Katie asked. "Let me go."

"Not till you tell me what's going on."

Angry, she whirled to face him. "What does it look like? I'm training—getting back in shape to run competitively."

"Does your doctor know? Your parents?"

"Who are you? My keeper?"

"I have a vested interest in your welfare, Katie," Josh insisted.

"Why? Because I'm toting around your brother's heart? It's *my* heart now."

He looked as if she'd slapped him, making her regret her cutting retort. "Look, Josh, I'm not mad at you. It's just that everybody keeps telling me what to do . . . what's best for me. I want to decide what's best for me. I'm not stupid, and I know how to take care of myself. I would never take unnecessary chances."

Josh stared down at her, fighting against hundreds of emotions bombarding him. "How long have you been working out?"

"About a week."

"You haven't told anyone, have you?"

Katie scraped the toe of her running shoe against the surface of the track. "I come at six-thirty, before Coach and any of the team members show up for their workouts."

He looked amazed. "How do you manage to sneak past your parents? I know how they guard you."

"It's easy—Mom's taken a job as a full-time sub-stitute for some teacher on maternity leave at an el-ementary school in the next county. She has to leave the house by six-fifteen to be on time. And Dad's been leaving around six every morning, try-ing to work extra hours."

Katie didn't tell Josh that her parents were hardly speaking to one another and that each seemed glad not to have to talk over the breakfast table as they had all their married life. Katie felt that their es-trangement was her fault. And that was another reason why she wanted to attend the Transplant Games. A vacation for the three of them in Los An-geles might make them feel like a family again.

"How do you get here?" Josh asked.

"I walk. I don't live that far from the school."

Josh groaned. "It's freezing cold that time of the morning."

"It's not so bad. Melody would pick me up and bring me if I asked her," Katie added. "I'm afraid that if she does, though, her mother will start ask-ing questions about why she has to be here thirty minutes earlier every day."

"Why didn't you ask me to come get you?"

Katie shrugged. "I guess because I figured you'd be against me, like everybody else."

Josh placed both hands on her shoulders, forcing her to look up at him. "It's not you against the rest of the world, Katie. All the people in your life care about you. They're concerned for you."

"I want to run in the Transplant Games," she said, hotly. "I have to be in condition in order to compete. If I compete, my parents will watch me and understand that I'm not some breakable doll—that I won't keel over dead because my heartbeat gets above sixty beats per minute."

"Is your doctor aware of your training program?"

This time, she held her temper. "Dr. Jacoby never said I couldn't train. He's a doctor, Josh . . . more concerned with his handiwork than with my happiness."

"What do you mean?"

"I'm a project for him. A case. A statistic."

"You told me that he was caring and understanding."

"He is—but—" She threw up her hands in exasperation. "I can't explain it. Doctors see people through the eyes of sickness. As long as a patient needs them, they give them one hundred percent attention. When a patient gets well, they move on to the next sick one."

"So, what's your point?"

Katie looked him squarely in the face. "I'm okay now—my heart's working fine. My body is healthy. I don't need him anymore . . . and he doesn't need to hover over me."

"He would want to know how you're caring for your body," Josh insisted.

"I told you, I follow a strict diet and exercise program set up by Barry. I'm simply accelerating the program a little bit so that I can attend the Transplant Games in July."

Josh gazed down at her, long and hard. "You

shouldn't be doing this alone. You should have a trainer."

The men's and women's track teams were beginning to trickle in for their preschool workouts. Katie saw Melody, Karen, and Pat walking out from the tunnel leading from the locker rooms. Her conversation with Josh had taken most of her workout time. "Are you volunteering?" she asked.

"Me?" He felt himself jolt at her suggestion. "I'm not a coach. I wouldn't know what to do if something happened to you."

Katie tossed her dark hair defiantly. "Look, I can't stand around debating this. Here's the bottom line: You can either help me train or stay out of my life." She turned toward the tunnel. "It's your choice, but whether you help or not, I'm training."

Sixteen

"So, what are the results of my latest biopsy? Is everything still fine?" Katie asked Dr. Jacoby. She purposefully sat on her hands to keep them from fluttering nervously. "Don't keep me in suspense."

Dr. Jacoby's brow furrowed as he flipped through the lab reports on his desk. "Hang on," he said.

Katie glanced over at her mother and noticed that her face looked pinched and drawn. She was anxious about the tests, too. The results of each biopsy became a benchmark for measuring the possibility of rejection.

Finally, Dr. Jacoby glanced up and smiled. "Perfect. Your tests look perfect. Not only the biopsy, but your treadmill and endurance tests, too." He peered at her over the top of his reading glasses.

"I'd say you seem to be as healthy as an athlete in strict training."

Katie felt a hot flash of color across her face. She gave her mother a sidelong glance, hoping her mom hadn't seen her look of guilt. "I've been following Barry's instructions," Katie replied cheerfully. "He's a great therapist." *And Josh is a terrific coach*, she added silently. After five months of working out, she was in great physical shape and close to her normal times on the thousand-and fifteen-hundred-meter race events—her specialties. In fact, she was almost back to her pre-illness condition in every respect.

Dr. Jacoby shut the file folder and laid it atop his desk. "What's on your mind, Katie?"

She was surprised that he'd picked up on her inner tension so readily. She sneaked another peek at her mother, then turned back to the doctor. "I still want to run in the Transplant Games in two months."

Katie felt her mother's instant disapproval when she asked, "Is that wise?"

Dr. Jacoby studied them both. "I have no medical reason for stopping you," he said carefully.

Katie felt her heart leap expectantly. "I can participate? It will be all right?"

"The Games are quite extraordinary. I've never attended them personally, but I've seen videotapes. Since the Kidney Foundation sponsors them, I know that medically, they're well supervised."

Katie was certain that his comments about medical safety were for her mother's sake, because she herself didn't need convincing. "It's like a mini-Olympics, isn't it?" she asked, also for her mother's benefit.

"Very much so. Except that there's competition at all levels. A participant doesn't have to be a fabulous athlete. There's even a walking event for those not in tip-top condition. Plus, there's a five-kilometer family fun race for both transplant patients and their families."

"A little something for everyone?" Katie's mother asked. Her voice sounded chilly, sarcastic.

"Volleyball, bowling, table tennis, swimming, track and field—to mention a few. The people who go seem to have a very good time," Dr. Jacoby said.

Katie's mother stood abruptly. "Thank you for the information. Now, if there's nothing else, I'd like to get Katie home."

Katie felt the keen edge of disappointment. She'd thought that Dr. Jacoby's strong endorsement of the games was approval for her to participate—maybe not at the level she desired to participate on, but approval nevertheless. Why was her mother being so stubborn? Didn't she understand what a good time they could all have together?

Her mother didn't speak about the visit to Dr. Jacoby's until they reached the house. Once inside, she tossed her keys onto the kitchen table and turned on Katie. "I don't appreciate your putting me on the spot the way you did in the doctor's office," she said.

"What do you mean?"

"The way you broached those Games with him,

the way you tried to manipulate him into endorsing your participating was unfair to me. You know how I feel about it."

Katie trooped to the refrigerator and poured herself a large glass of orange juice. "I'd be hard-pressed *not* to know how you feel. You scowl every time I mention the Games. I want to go, Mom. I want you and Dad to come, too. Dr. Jacoby approves of them, and you heard him say that I was in good shape."

"I heard him say what *you* wanted to hear."

Katie banged her glass down on the countertop. "I've sent away for the registration forms and called about airline tickets. I can pay all our expenses with my Wish money."

Her mother's mouth dropped open. "Your Wish money? Is that how you're planning to waste it—is that how you're going to piddle it away? On silly, insignificant things instead of the important things in your life?"

Her mother's reaction surprised Katie. They hadn't discussed the money since before her operation. "You once said for me to spend it on something I wanted. Something exciting for all of us to do together. The trip won't cost too much. There'll be plenty left over. One hundred thousand dollars is a lot of money."

"You bet it's a lot of money," her mother snapped. "Money that can be put to a good cause—like college, or medical bills."

"Dad said his insurance covered my transplant."

"Your operation, yes—but it's not going to cover

your immune-suppressant drugs after the first year."

Shocked to learn that her father's insurance coverage would be running out, Katie said, "I take a lot of pills. I can't live without them."

"That's right. And every one of those pills is expensive. A year's worth is going to cost us around ten thousand dollars. Think of it. Ten thousand dollars annually! That's why your father and I are working so hard. And now you come to me and say you want to zip off to play in some silly games. That Wish money can mean years of medication for you, Katie. Why don't you think about spending it to keep yourself alive instead of frittering it away on foolishness?"

"I didn't know . . ." Katie stammered. "I didn't mean to cost you and Dad so much money. I'm sorry . . . really sorry . . ."

Suddenly, her mother looked stricken and ashamed. She placed her hand over her mouth and began to cry softly. She stepped away from the table, came over to Katie, and scooped her into her arms. "Oh, baby, forgive me," she pleaded. "I should have never told you that. I'd pay a million dollars, and scrub floors to earn it, in order to keep you alive. I'm sorry I sounded off. I didn't mean a word of it. Please, forget I said anything about money. Your father and I've been under such pressure lately."

Katie remembered the argument she'd overheard months before and realized that her parents had never truly resolved their differences. The additional news about the loss of insurance benefits must be putting an additional burden on them. "I had no idea my pills cost so much money," Katie said.

Her mother pulled away and looked deeply into Katie's eyes. "I don't care about the money. All that's important is *you*," she insisted. "I'm afraid the Games might be dangerous for you."

Surely, JWC had known about the expense in keeping a transplant patient alive, Katie thought. That's probably why she'd been selected to receive a check in the first place. Yet, even though that idea crossed Katie's mind, she simultaneously recalled something JWC had said in the letter: "Use my gift to fulfill your wish." Deep down, she knew she didn't want to spend *all* her money on immune-suppressant medications, nor did she believe her benefactor would have wanted her to.

Katie grasped her mother's hands. "Mom, don't you see what's happened to us? We've all become so involved with my medical problems that we've not taken any time to 'stop and smell the roses.'" Katie used one of her grandmother's favorite phrases. "I agree—I should use some of the money to help with my medical expenses."

"Honey, no—"

Katie ignored her mother's interruption. "Wait. Hear me out. I want to help. But I also want to spend some of it on having a good time. I really think that's why JWC gave me the money in the first place. Whoever this person is, he or she understands what it's like to be sick enough to die. I figure that's why JWC gives money away—so that people who are sick can have some fun."

Katie's tone had grown passionate. "You know, Mom, until this happened to me, I didn't appreciate what a sick person has to go through day by day. I didn't appreciate living until I almost died."

Tears shimmered in her mother's eyes. "I never want to have to go through the fear of losing you again."

"Maybe you won't," Katie said. "We don't know, because no one can see the future. All I know is that right now, I'm alive and well and happy. And I want us all to go to the Games, and I want to run again competitively. I won't hurt myself. I'll be sensible and careful. If you and Daddy are with me, I'll *have* to be, won't I?"

Her mother smiled sheepishly. "Your father tells me I'm much too protective."

"If you got any closer, we'd be Siamese twins," Katie said, mixing the truth with humor.

"I get your point." Her mother fumbled for a paper napkin and wiped her eyes. "So, you've checked everything out for the Games?" she asked in resignation.

"The travel agent I talked to is working up a package deal—flight, hotel, the works."

"For the three of us?"

Katie hesitated briefly before plunging ahead. "Actually, for us and for Josh, too. I think he should come—and Gramps if he wants. But Josh for sure. He loved Aaron so much, and it would be pretty special to him if he could see me run."

Her mother nodded. "You're right, of course. He deserves to come. In a roundabout way, he's the reason you're alive."

Katie gave her mother a hug. "Why don't you call Daddy and tell him we're going on a vacation? Then I'll call Josh and the travel agent. We're going to have the time of our lives, Mom—thanks to someone whose identity I don't even know."

Seventeen

"How's your room? Do you like it? Are you having a good time?" Katie was all but dancing in the corridor of the luxury hotel as she fired questions at Josh.

"Quit bobbing around," Josh said with a laugh. "You're giving me motion sickness." He propped his arms over her shoulders to settle her down. "My room's fine. And yours?"

"The best. Mom and Dad's is nice, too."

"You got everybody a separate room?"

"How many kids would want to bunk with their parents?" Katie made a face to underscore her point. "Too bad Gramps didn't come," she added.

"It meant a lot to him that you asked, but between us, I think the trip would have been too much for him. He said, 'If the Good Lord wanted people to fly, he'd have given them wings instead of arms.' "

Katie laughed at Josh's perfect imitation of Gramps's voice. "Also, I think he was afraid to leave his rose garden for too long," Josh said.

"Well, anyway, you came," Katie said. When she'd first asked him, he'd been hesitant.

"I have to work this summer," he'd told her. "I need to save money for school."

She'd assured him that the trip would cost him nothing and had told him about the Wish money—which greatly impressed him. "The trip's my treat," she had insisted. "And we'll only be gone four days. You've got the rest of the summer to work."

Looking down at her in the hallway, Josh could hardly believe that they were actually in Los Angeles. "Melody wanted to come, too, but she had some special family reunion coming up," Katie said.

"This way, I won't have to share you," Josh replied, and winked.

"As I've had to share you with my father," Katie teased. "The two of you talked during the whole flight."

"I like your dad." Josh found Katie's father easy to like. 'He talked to him like an adult, asked his opinion, and respected it when Josh gave it. If only he had a father like Mr. O'Roark . . .

"My dad was pretty impressed with your track season," Katie said. "Ann Arbor will be a contender for State next year."

"The girls' team would have done better if you could have run."

"Next year," Katie declared. "When I'm a senior, I'll be back on the team."

"It seems to me you do everything you set your mind on, Katie."

"Daddy says it's nothing but Irish bullheadedness and that it's a very unfeminine trait." She tipped her chin upward and grinned. "Maybe he's right."

Josh wanted to tell her that she was anything but unfeminine or unattractive. When he'd first started training with her months before, he'd done so partly out of fear for her life, fear of losing his one link to Aaron. Josh wasn't sure when his feelings began to change, he only knew that they had changed. Being with Katie was a constant adventure—a six-month joyride for him. Her determination, her grit, her dedication impressed him. She'd worked harder than anyone he'd ever seen to get in shape for the Transplant Games. Only Josh knew that she hadn't come merely to coast around a track for appearance's sake. Katie O'Roark had come to win. He felt a little guilty for not sharing his knowledge with her parents, but his first loyalty was to Katie, and he knew she'd worked too hard to have anything abort her grand scheme.

"Are you listening to me, Josh?"

Katie's question quickly dragged Josh out of his thoughts. "Sure." His face flushed. "What did you say?"

Katie punched his arm. "I said that according to

the brochure, there's going to be a big fiesta with dancing tonight. Doesn't that sound like fun?"

"What's a fiesta?"

"A party, silly! Can you dance?"

He rocked back on his heels. "You'll just have to wait and find out."

She shoved him playfully and darted quickly inside her hotel room before he could retaliate. "See you tonight," she called. "And you'd better know how to dance, buster!"

The fiesta was held on the UCLA campus, outside, under the stars. The smells of sizzling ribs and chicken filled the air, and colored lanterns swung over tables draped in checkered cloths. Music from a Mexican band, playing in front of a wooden dance floor set up on the grass, floated above laughter from groups of people gathered on the sprawling lawn.

"I never dreamed there'd be so many people," Katie heard her mother say as they crossed the grassy field.

Katie, holding Josh's hand, felt euphoric. The number of people amazed her, too. Everybody looked so normal, so healthy. She couldn't begin to even guess which ones were organ recipients like herself. The four of them chose seats at a table with several strangers, and after a round of introductions, Katie knew that she was sharing dinner with a heart-lung, a liver, and two kidney transplant recipients. She discovered that these people were much like herself—very grateful to donors and their families, without whom, they would all be dead.

Beside her, Josh remained quiet as the others shared their stories. After a while, she leaned over and asked him, "How about that dance?"

The dance floor was full, but Katie hardly noticed. In Josh's arms, she felt as if they were all alone. "Did the conversation depress you?" she asked intuitively.

"A little," he admitted. "I feel kind of strange being here. None of the others seemed to know who their donors were, like you do."

"It sounded to me as if some of them wanted to, though."

"Are you glad you do?" His gaze was serious, and Katie stopped swaying with the music.

"You know I am."

"When I looked at them, I couldn't help wondering if any of them might hold parts of Aaron." She could tell he was troubled, and unable to put into words what he was feeling. "Can we take a walk?" he asked.

"Let me tell my parents," Katie said. She scanned the crowded floor and saw them standing at a far corner. Her mother was wrapped in her dad's arms, her eyes closed, her head resting on his shoulder. He was holding her tightly, stroking her hair with one hand. They seemed to be dancing to music only they could hear.

"I don't think they'll miss us," Josh said.

"Me, either." The picture of them warmed Katie. They looked happy together once again.

Katie walked with Josh across the lawn, away from the buildings, and into a cluster of trees. The sounds from the band grew fainter, and above, through the branches of pine trees, she could see the stars, spread out like diamonds on black velvet. When they stopped, Josh angled himself against a tree trunk. He took hold of both her hands.

"You still miss Aaron, don't you?" Katie asked, breaking the silence, urging him to talk about his feelings.

"It's been hard without him, all right. He was my big brother, and he took care of me."

"The way you take care of me?"

A ghost of a smile crossed Josh's face. "He never nagged the way I do." Josh sobered. "Katie, Aaron was more than my brother. He was more like my father."

Katie's heart thudded. She'd wondered about his family a million times. "How so? Did he help raise you?"

"He protected me."

"From what?"

"Not everybody has parents who care the way yours do, Katie."

"You had a bad home life?" The idea was foreign to her.

"Both my parents are alcoholics." He took a long, shuddering breath. "Pop beat up on Mom all the time."

Horrified, Katie asked, "You and Aaron, too?"

"No—just her. Over the years, I lost all respect for her because she wouldn't leave him, not even now, when she can. It's like a trap she can't get out

of . . . that she doesn't want out of. I don't understand her, or him."

Josh shook his head to clear out the painful
memories. "Whenever she wound up in the hospital, Aaron took care of the two of us. He cooked,
did laundry . . . whatever needed doing."

"It's hard to believe you had a violent home life.
You're so gentle, Josh."

He looked into her eyes. "That's Aaron's doing,
too. He tried to stick up for Mom. He used to tell
me that we shouldn't ever think beating up on
somebody was okay. When he was fifteen, he
started going to Al-Anon meetings, and he took me
with him." Katie knew vaguely that Al-Anon was
the support group for families of alcoholics.
"There, we both learned how not to be like our father."

Katie's heart was breaking for him. No wonder
the loss of Aaron had been so difficult for him!
He'd lost his only true family when Aaron died.
"You're the most wonderful person I know, Josh."

He toyed with the flower behind her ear. "I wish
Aaron could have known you. I wish he could have
known where his heart ended up."

"He does," she whispered. Without taking her
eyes from Josh's face, she lifted his hand and
placed it gently beneath her left breast, against the
top of her ribcage. She knew he could feel the distinct thumping of her heart, just as she was feeling
it. "This heart is only an organ, Josh. A very special
pump, issued at birth to every living being. The
person of Aaron isn't alive inside this piece of tis-

sue. He's alive inside *you*. You're the one keeping Aaron alive, not me. And so long as you remember him, he'll always be alive."

Josh concentrated on the throb of Katie's beating heart beneath his palm, the warmth of her skin through the fabric of her blouse. Without taking his gaze from her beautiful face, he said, "I love you, Katie."

"And I love you." She knew it was true. She loved Josh Martel from the depths of her soul.

"I have a present for you," he said.

"For me?"

He reached into his pocket and pulled out a small, flat box. Eagerly, she tore off the paper and raised the lid. The moonlight caught on a thin silver chain holding a heart-shaped locket. "I thought you could add it to your heart collection," he said. "Along with Aaron's and mine."

Katie felt tears swimming in her eyes. "It's so beautiful. Thank you." She could scarcely breathe as he fastened it around her neck.

"This is really for tomorrow," he said. "After you win that race." Josh slipped his arms around her and lowered his lips to hers.

Katie held her breath, closed her eyes, and savored the sensation of his mouth against hers. "Is it like kissing your brother?" she teased, pulling slightly back.

"Not even close," he told her, then kissed her again.

Eighteen

Katie walked around the track in the Parade of Athletes, waving at cheering fans. She felt the sun's warmth on her head and shoulders, and the soft summer breeze in her hair. Seeing her fellow competitors dressed in bright, colorful athletic gear filled her with an overwhelming sense of pride and exuberance. *I made it!* she told herself. *Thank you, JWC.* Because of the One Last Wish Foundation, in a few hours she would be competing against some fifteen other female athletes in the thousand-meter foot race.

She waved to the crowd as her gaze drifted upward to the Olympic torch positioned high above the stands, directly below the scoreboard of the UCLA stadium. Minutes before, a ten-year-old kidney recipient had run from the tunnel, carrying a lighted flare. Katie could still feel the remains of the lump in her throat as she'd watched the boy jog around the track, sprint up the stairs, and light the flame, signifying the start of the Games.

As she rounded the final turn of the parade, she saw Josh hanging over the wall of the stands. Elsewhere in the crowd, she knew her parents were watching. They had come to breakfast that morning in the hotel restaurant smiling contentedly, causing Katie and Josh to exchange sly, knowing glances. Katie realized that at some point during the previous night, they'd resolved all their differences. She was grateful to JWC for that, too.

Once the parade broke up and the various events began, Josh leapt down from the wall and came over to her. "You doing all right?" he asked.

"I'm nervous."

He draped a towel around her neck. "The way I figure it, you've only got about three serious contenders in your race. One woman's from Maine, and she's very good. She's an international runner with a lot of visibility."

Katie's heart sank. She'd known when she'd elected to run in the senior women's category instead of the junior one that it would be tough going, but she'd wanted to really test herself, not just take a win. "And the others?" she asked.

"They're of similar caliber—very good and very seasoned."

"I'm not going to change categories," Katie said.

"I didn't expect you to. I'm only telling you what you're up against. These women have run in this race before, and the one from Maine, Fran Bonita, won the Outstanding Female Athlete Award for this entire Olympics last year."

"Where do people get the idea that transplant recipients are invalids?" Katie grumbled, shaking her head. "I'll bet some of these athletes could outdo some of the country's professional, 'normal' ones."

"I'll bet you're right," Josh said with a grin. "I'm glad I'm not competing—I'd probably get whipped."

Katie heard her father hail her from the stands. She followed the wall along the track, stopped, and looked up at him. "You need anything?" her dad asked.

"I'm fine, Dad," Katie said, her tone more patient than her attitude. "Josh is keeping an eye on me."

"I figure that your race will wrap up in time for me to fax my column back to the paper," he told her with a smile.

"You're going to write about this?" Katie tried to sound piqued, but secretly, she was pleased.

"You bet I'm writing about it. The whole world needs to know about these athletes."

"And if I just *happen* to win a race . . . ?"

"I'll give you a quick mention." He shrugged innocently.

"Oh, Daddy!"

He laughed and headed back up to join his wife.

Josh touched her arm. "You'd better start warming up. Your race is up soon."

By the time her race was called, Katie's muscles

were limber, but her stomach was tied in knots. She paced the infield, while Josh encouraged her with a pep talk. "Don't try to set the pace. Hang back and see how the others are running. When you hear that bell lap, you've got to have plenty in reserve. Just remember to kick high all the way to the wire. You're good, Katie, and I think you can win."

"Do you really think I'm good? You've never told me that before."

"I've only seen you run against the clock, but I know you're good—I've read your father's columns." His honey-brown eyes twinkled mischievously.

She slugged his arm. "Wait until I'm a famous runner. Then you'll wish you'd been nicer to me."

Josh's expression sobered. "You're going to do just fine out there. Remember, you've got a tradition to uphold. Aaron was an athlete, too, so I know you have an athlete's heart—in more ways than one."

Katie raised up and kissed Josh quickly. "Thanks, Coach—see you at the finish line."

As Josh watched her jog toward the track, his stomach knotted. She'd worked so hard these past several months, but he had no way of knowing how she would do. He only hoped that she'd run well and not affect her transplanted heart in any way. He realized that he'd been more than her coach for her training process. He'd been her accomplice. If anything happened to her during this race, he wouldn't be able to live with himself.

"Hang in there, Katie," he whispered to himself. "And go for the gold."

Katie tied her long hair into a ponytail, making certain that her bangs were well off her face. Perspiration trickled down between her shoulder blades. She was more nervous for this race than for any race she'd ever run in high school, including the district finals in her sophomore year.

As she continued to keep her muscles limber, she cut her eyes sideways toward her opponents. Fran Bonita of Maine was a standout. She was lean and hard-limbed, a fine running machine in prime physical condition. Katie took a deep breath. What had she been thinking about when she'd decided to run in the senior women's division? She couldn't compete seriously with grown women!

A track official blew his whistle and beckoned the runners to the starting line. Katie glanced toward the stands. A sea of cheering faces greeted her, and she felt her adrenaline surge. "In three minutes, it will be all over," she told herself, taking her place on the line. Months of training all came down to this moment.

Not all the runners were serious about winning, Katie reminded herself. Some were running simply to say that they had competed. They would be easy to beat. Katie leaned forward, holding her breath. She heard her blood pounding in her ears. She felt like a cat, sleek and taut, ready to test the wind. She knew she was fit, knew that her heart was strong and capable. Eyes straight ahead, she stared down the track to the first turn, plotting her race strategy. The starter's gun went off, the crowd roared, and Katie sprang forward.

She quickly settled into her pace, allowing others to pass her, believing the leaders would burn out before the finish. The pack rounded the first turn and stretched out in a line. Katie controlled her breathing, holding the air in her lungs and then releasing it from her diaphragm. She refused to check on her opponents, knowing it could undermine her own race. From the corner of her eye, she saw a woman coming on strong. *Take it easy,* she warned herself. It wasn't Fran.

Katie concentrated on the feel of her running shoes pounding the surface of the track. She swung her arms and kept her body under rigid mental control. The wind whipped her face, her breaths came fast and deep. The crowd and its noise evaporated as she focused all her energy on the race.

She came around the track twice, continuing to gauge her pace, holding back, reining in, saving herself for the final surge that must come down the stretch for the finish line. Timing was everything. Too fast and she'd burn out, have nothing left in reserve. Not fast enough and she'd fall too far behind to catch the leaders. Mentally, she heard Josh's voice from all her months of training. "Hold back," he'd shout. Or "Pump, pump!"

The din of the bell lap sounded, and Katie knew it was time to make her move. She reached deep and stretched further. She pulled past the front-runner and cut to the inside lane. She could see the finish line, could feel the victory, when from out of nowhere, she saw the flying arms of Fran Bonita. She was going to catch her, pass her. Katie felt a moment of panic. She was giving all she had, and still the woman beside her was pulling ahead.

"Reach, Katie, reach!" Through a haze, she heard Josh's voice loud and strong. She ran hard. Her lungs screamed in protest, but Katie paid them no heed. She felt her heart pounding, and in that moment, she saw the face of Aaron Martel in her mind's eye. He was grinning, as in his graduation photo, urging her on, propelling her forward. Suddenly, it was as if she'd grown wings. Katie pressed her body forward, and like an arrow splitting the wind, her chest hit the tape a full length in front of her opponent.

Nineteen

As she crossed the finish line, Katie heard the roar of the crowd through the rushing surge of blood in her ears. A track official hurried over to her, his stopwatch in his hand. "Are you all right, girl? I think you broke some records! What a sensational race!"

Katie gasped for air, nodding, trying to clear her head and regain control of her pounding heart. Suddenly, she was caught from behind, spun, and scooped up in Josh's arms. "You won, Katie! You won, big-time!"

She tried to smile, but her legs felt rubbery and she couldn't catch her breath.

"Give her some room," Josh yelled to the crowd gathering around her. He walked with her, rubbing her shoulders and wrapping a wet towel over her neck. "You okay?"

"Never better," Katie managed between puffs of air. "It felt so good, Josh. So good to run. I didn't think I was going to pull ahead in the stretch, but then I thought about Aaron, and it was as if he were with me. He gave me that extra edge to punch through."

Josh squeezed her shoulders. "*You* did it, Katie. It was your race, your heart."

She felt someone nudge her and turned to see a sweat-streaked Fran Bonita. The woman held out her hand. "You were awesome," Fran said. "I've run in a lot of races and faced some keen competition. I never expected to face a runner of your caliber at a place like the Transplant Games. Congratulations."

Katie shook her hand, feeling dazzled. "You were a great incentive," she said.

"I hope to meet you on the track again."

"Next year!" she called as Fran walked away.

Fran turned and grinned. "For sure."

Katie saw her parents rushing toward her. For a moment, she chilled, unsure of how they were going to react. Her mother threw her arms around her. "You were wonderful! Absolutely wonderful!"

"You aren't mad?"

"I'm furious, but what can I do about it?" Her mother was smiling and crying at the same time. "I'm so proud of you, honey. You always said you were born to run." She hugged Katie again.

Her father ruffled her hair, his face a beaming

smile. "You're some runner, Katie O'Roark. It's official—you came within two-tenths of the women's collegiate record for the thousand-meter. And you're only sixteen! I'm speechless."

"I doubt that!" Katie said, laughing.

Later, when she stood on the platform for the medal ceremony, Katie's eyes swept the crowd. This time, she picked out her parents instantly. They were holding a banner that read: KATIE GOT THE GOLD. She grinned.

Josh stood below the platform on the bright green grass. He gave her a thumbs-up as the officials slipped the gold medal around her neck. Katie knew it wasn't a real gold medal like from the official Olympics, but nothing could convince her that it meant any less. For an instant, she felt time stand still as she savored the sweetness of her victory, then she raised both arms above her head, and the crowd went wild with cheering.

The next evening at the closing banquet, Katie felt pangs of regret. "It's hard to believe it's all over," she remarked to Josh and her parents.

"We've all had a great time," her mother said. "I'm very glad we came." She and Katie exchanged looks of understanding, each remembering their argument about the Wish money. Wherever JWC was, Katie hoped he or she knew how much joy the money had given to Katie and her family. She still longed to meet her benefactor, but was certain by this time that she never would. For whatever reason, JWC had chosen to remain anonymous. Silently, Katie wished her secret philanthropist the best that life could bring.

"Are you Katie O'Roark?"

The man's question snapped Katie from her musings. She looked up to see a large, heavyset man. "Yes, I am."

"I'm Phil Stoner, women's track coach at Arizona State." He nodded greetings to Josh and her parents. "I was pretty impressed by what I saw you do on the track yesterday."

Katie smiled. "Thanks—I love to run."

"That was obvious," he said with a laugh. "The Good Lord made you fast, Katie, and medical science gave you a new life."

"A heart," she said, wondering if he, too, was a transplant recipient.

Almost as if he'd read her mind, the coach added, "My son over there got a kidney eight years ago." He motioned toward a man in his thirties, sitting with a young woman and three little girls. "Jim was dying. He'd been on dialysis for two years, but his kidneys continued to fail. He was leaving behind his family, his whole future."

"He was fortunate to find a donor," Katie said.

"I was his donor," Phil told her with a beaming smile. "It was the greatest feeling in the world— knowing that I could give my son a second chance at life."

Katie felt goose bumps skitter along her arms.

"I support the Transplant Games wholeheartedly," Phil went on. "The world needs to know that people with organ transplants are very normal peo-

ple, grateful to be alive. Anyway, when I came this
year, I never imagined I'd see the race I saw yesterday. I want you to keep in touch with me."

Her eyes grew wide. "Do you think I could get a
scholarship for track? Even with a heart transplant?"

The coach laughed. "You'd be the secret weapon
of some collegiate coach's arsenal, Katie. Of course,
you could. Coaches pick athletes who can win.
And you're a winner."

She felt Josh reach under the table and grasp her
hand. "We're all winners," she replied, squeezing
his in return.

Later, during the banquet, when special awards
were given out, Katie received one for Best New
Participant. She cradled it in her arms, knowing it
would get a place of honor on the shelves in her
bedroom. Afterward, she hugged other recipients
warmly, promising to return to the Games next
year and run in more races.

"It's hard to say good-bye," Katie confided to
Josh as they returned to their hotel.

"There's always next year," he said.

Katie didn't remind him that for some of them,
there would be no next year. For in spite of their
good health, medications, doctors, tests, and tech-
nological advancements, all of them were carrying
around foreign organs inside their bodies—organs
that could reject at any time, leaving them in desperate need of a new donor, or dead.

At noon the next day, Katie, Josh, and her parents boarded a plane and flew home to Michigan.

*   *   *

Once home, in spite of her reluctance, Katie became a minicelebrity. The paper did a front-page story on her, two TV stations invited her to be a guest on special programs devoted to community events, and several radio stations did live interviews with her.

"You look fabulous on the tube," Melody told her as she spent one rainy afternoon in Katie's bedroom, hearing all about Los Angeles. "Maybe I could be your groupie."

"Very funny. I'm only doing this to help give publicity to the organ donation program. You know how I hate this limelight stuff."

Melody made a face. "Party pooper. Has Oprah called yet?"

Katie bopped her on the head with a pillow, sending the two of them rolling and giggling on the floor.

"You are returning to dull Ann Arbor High in the fall, aren't you?" Melody asked after their tussle.

"You bet. We're going to take state honors in track this year."

"I think we can," Melody agreed. She paused, before asking, "How are you and Josh?"

Katie fingered the silver locket around her neck. "Crazy about each other. Melly, I feel like the luckiest person in the world."

That night, when Josh came over, she took him outside to the swing on her front porch. They sat close together while the soft scents of the summer night folded around them and fireflies blinked from the front lawn. Katie handed him a large, flat box, which she plucked from its hiding place under a nearby table. "Now, it's my turn to give you a present," she said.

"For me?" He looked genuinely surprised.

"For posterity," she teased mysteriously. He opened the box and lifted out a large scrapbook. "I've been working on it for months."

Josh flipped it open. His breath caught. She'd written a dedication page, which read: "To the Life and Courage of Aaron Martel." Every page was filled, not only with the photos he had lent her, but with other photographs and with newspaper clippings about Aaron's high school and brief collegiate athletic careers. A large knot of emotion wedged in Josh's throat. When he was able to clear it out, he asked, "Where did you get all this stuff?"

"Your gramps helped get the extra pictures for me, and Daddy helped with the articles. He got them from your newspaper back in Indiana, from their old files. And the coach at Michigan is a friend of Dad's, so he was able to supply the college information. I left some pages blank in the back in case you want to add any personal stuff." She reached out and stroked his cheek with the back of her hand. "Do you like it? Are you surprised?"

To answer her, he put the book aside, took her in his arms, and kissed her with all the feeling he had stored up and locked away in his heart throughout his lifetime.

*   *   *

In the middle of the night, Katie awoke feeling chilled and disoriented. Her teeth chattered, and her head hurt. She pulled the covers up to her chin, thinking that maybe the air conditioner was malfunctioning, but she couldn't get warm. The next morning, when her mother came to check on her, Katie was huddled beneath the covers.

Her mother took one look at her and blanched. "Katie, what's wrong?"

Tears filled Katie's eyes, and fear filled her mind. "I'm sick, Mom," she said. "You'd better call the doctor."

Twenty

"It's a flu virus," Dr. Jacoby said. He stood at the side of Katie's hospital bed, examining lab reports.

"The flu's pretty common," Katie said, hopefully. "You should have me up and around in no time, shouldn't you?"

The worried expressions on her parents' faces were upsetting her. She wanted to chase away their fears, so she selected the words of assurance she longed to hear from her doctor. Dr. Jacoby continued to frown. "No illness is simple for you, Katie. Remember, you're taking immune-suppressants, and they make you highly susceptible to sickness and infections."

Yet without the suppressants, her heart would certainly reject. Katie felt caught in a vicious cycle.

"What about the results of her heart biopsy?" Her mother asked the question Katie had feared asking.

Dr. Jacoby glanced up from Katie's medical chart. "It's showing mild rejection."

Katie felt sick to her stomach. "That's bad, isn't it?" she asked.

"While rejection is always a threat, episodes aren't uncommon when a patient undergoes an infection or illness, such as you're experiencing."

"What are you going to do about it?"

"We'll increase your immune-suppressant doses and see if that doesn't turn it around."

"And if it doesn't?" Katie persisted.

"Let's not borrow trouble." Dr. Jacoby patted her arm.

Katie felt coldness snake along her insides. She understood that a second heart transplant was unlikely for her both because of the scarcity of donor hearts and because of her blood type. Aaron's heart had come to her through an odd chain of events that wouldn't likely be repeated. Also, Katie realized that while a kidney patient who rejected could go back on dialysis, there was no magical machine capable of keeping her alive until a new donor could be found—there was no mechanical substitute for the human heart.

As upset as her parents were, nothing prepared Katie for the degree of Josh's anguish. When he came to see her, he looked terrified. She wanted to assure him that she'd be all right, but knew she couldn't lie. He took her hand and held it tightly, as if his grip might pull her away from the darkness threatening her. "Don't leave me, Katie," he whispered.

Weak as she was, she reached up and smoothed the hair on his forehead. "No regrets, okay?"

"Why, Katie? Everything was going so perfect— why did this have to happen?"

"I don't know." She moistened her lips. She felt weak and feverish, and it was difficult to concentrate, but there was something she wanted Josh to know. "If I had it all to do over again, I would. Every bit of it. The surgery . . . the pain . . . the fear . . . the recovery . . . the isolation—all of it was worth it, Josh, because it gave me another shot at life."

Josh started to speak, but she silenced him with a look. "Hear me out. Every day, every minute that I've had, has been wonderful. I wouldn't trade it for anything, and I'd do it all again if I got the chance. Think of it, Josh. I've been living—really living—with another person's heart inside my chest for almost a year. Isn't that extraordinary?"

Josh watched her eyes shut as she slipped into a world of dreams where he couldn't go. He held her hand and struggled with bone-chilling fear. "Stay with me," he whispered, remembering what his grandfather had told him the night of Aaron's funeral. You'll be happy again, the old man had said. He'd been right. The months Josh had spent with Katie had been some of the happiest of his life.

A person never grows deep unless he's been through suffering. Gramps had told Josh that, too. *Right again,* Josh thought. At the moment, he felt a thousand feet deep. He brought Katie's hand to his mouth and kissed her palm. "Hang in there, Katie. Hang in."

Increased doses of her regular medications didn't halt the rejection process. "Don't you have any secret, magic microbes, Doc?" Katie asked a frowning Dr. Jacoby.

"There is another drug," Dr. Jacoby said, his eyes serious. "It's experimental, though. We use it only in extreme cases, when conventional medications aren't doing the trick. It's called by a string of letters and numbers. We can't use it for long, because of the side effects, but sometimes, it turns the tide and halts the rejection. Then we switch back to the tried and true as soon as we have a particular episode under control."

Katie saw her parents exchange glances. Weakly, she said, "It's my life. I want to give it a try."

"Oh, Katie—" her mother started to protest.

Katie's dad put his arm around his wife's shoulders. "If that's what Katie wants, we shouldn't interfere," he said.

Her mother nodded, without an argument. Katie knew the matter was out of all of their hands, anyway. She looked at her doctor. "Let's do it."

"You'll run a high fever," Dr. Jacoby cautioned. "You'll be very sick . . . disoriented and out of it. You might even have to go back on a ventilator for a time. But if it works—"

"Do it," Katie repeated, holding his gaze unflinchingly. "You know me—I have to go for the gold."

"We'll have to move you back into the ICU."

Katie hated the thought, but knew she had no choice. She looked to her parents. "I want you to promise me something."

"Anything," her dad said.

"If it doesn't work, promise me you'll look out for Josh . . . that you'll take care of him, be a family to him."

"We'll treat him like a son," her father said.

"And the rest of the Wish money . . . see that it goes to someone in need of a transplant who can't afford it."

"If that's what you want."

"It's what I want." Katie shut her eyes, too exhausted to say anything else.

Josh sat out on the hospital patio, under a striped umbrella, sipping a soda and staring down at the concrete. The soda tasted flat, and the umbrella was doing little to hold back the heat of the August sun. He felt as if he were in purgatory—the state of torment between heaven and hell. *Eight days.* Katie had been in a coma for eight days while the doctors pumped her full of some new potion that didn't seem to be working.

Josh wouldn't have come down for a soda, preferring to keep his vigil in the ICU waiting room, but Mrs. O'Roark had insisted. "Take a break, Josh, while Dr. Jacoby's in with her. You know I'll come get you if anything changes."

Day after day, Katie lay on the bed, with ma-
doing the work of her lungs, and her kidneys

failing. Josh thought back to Aaron, but Aaron had been brain dead. With Katie it was different. It was, wasn't it? Her heart—when had he stopped thinking of it as Aaron's heart?—kept beating. "It can turn around," Dr. Jacoby kept telling them. "I've seen it before in patients sicker than Katie."

Something embedded in the surface of the concrete caught Josh's eye. A plant had pushed up through a crack in the stone. He leaned closer, squinting. Actually, the green stem had cracked the cement in its quest for the sun. The tiny plant caught his imagination.

How miraculous life was! Why, it could even move stone when it was programmed to grow. The idea caused him to suck in his breath. Ever since his childhood, he'd heard it said that life was fragile. Staring down at the sturdy plant made him pause, made him see the issue of life in a new and different light. Life was hardy. It was tenacious. Life couldn't be defeated. He started to pluck the stem, but stopped himself. It had fought its way through solid concrete. He couldn't snuff it out.

Aaron had died, but his death had given Katie life. She, in her way, had given life to Josh. Even if death took her, it couldn't snuff her out, just as it couldn't eradicate Aaron, just as it couldn't eliminate anyone who had once lived. Life was a gift. The realization swept over Josh and he felt renewed hope.

Josh leapt up. He had to see Katie. He had to touch her, let her know that even if she went away now, he'd see her again. He ran into the hospital lobby, but didn't wait for the elevator. He took the stairs up to the ninth floor, running so fast that he arrived at the ICU completely out of breath.

"Are you all right?" Katie's startled mother asked.

"She's going to make it, Mrs. O'Roark," Josh said between gasps. "One way or the other, Katie's going to make it."

"Oh, Josh, if we could only be sure." She seemed eager to match his optimism.

"I just saw a plant coming up through a solid slab of concrete," he explained. "I'm telling you, it was coming straight up to the sun, straight up to the sky. We have to believe she'll make it."

Dear Reader,

$\mathcal{F}$or those of you who have been longtime readers, I hope you have enjoyed this One Last Wish volume. For those of you discovering One Last Wish for the first time, I hope you will want to read the other books that are listed in detail in the next few pages. From Lacey to Katie to Morgan and the rest, you'll discover the lives of the characters I hope you've come to care about just as I have.

Since the series began, I have received numerous letters from teens wishing to volunteer at Jenny House. That is not possible because Jenny House exists only in my imagination, but there are many fine organizations and camps for sick kids that would welcome volunteers. If you are interested in becoming such a volunteer, contact your local hospitals about their volunteer programs or try calling service organizations in your area to find out how you can help. Your own school might have a list of community service programs.

Extending yourself is one of the best ways of expanding your world . . . and of enlarging your heart. Turning good intentions into actions is consistently one of the most rewarding experiences in life. My wish is that the ideals of Jenny House will be carried on by you, my reader. I hope that now that we share the Jenny House attitude, you will believe as I do that the end is often only the beginning.

Thank you for caring.

You'll want to read all the One Last Wish
books by bestselling author

Let Him Live
Someone Dies, Someone Lives
Mother, Help Me Live
A Time to Die
Sixteen and Dying
Mourning Song
The Legacy: Making Wishes Come True
Please Don't Die
She Died Too Young
All the Days of Her Life
A Season for Goodbye
Reach for Tomorrow

*I*F YOU WANT TO KNOW MORE ABOUT MEGAN,

BE SURE TO READ

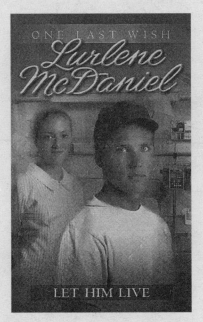

ON SALE NOW FROM BANTAM BOOKS
0-553-56067-0

Excerpt from *Let Him Live* by Lurlene McDaniel
Copyright © 1993 by Lurlene McDaniel

Published by Bantam Doubleday Dell Books for Young Readers
a division of Random House, Inc.
1540 Broadway, New York, New York 10036

*B*eing a candy striper isn't Megan Charnell's idea of an exciting summer, but she volunteered and can't get out of it. Megan has her own problems to deal with. Still, when she meets Donovan Jacoby, she find herself getting involved in his life.

Donovan shares with Megan his secret: An anonymous benefactor has granted him one last wish, and he needs Megan's help. The money can't buy a compatible transplant, but it can allow Donovan to give his mother and little brother something he feels he owes them. Can Megan help make his dream come true?

"When I first got sick in high school, kids were pretty sympathetic, but the sicker I got and the more school I missed, the harder it was to keep up with the old crowd," Donovan explained. "Some of them tried to understand what I was going through, but unless you've been really sick . . ." He didn't finish the sentence.

"I've never been sick," Meg said, "but I really do know what you're talking about."

He tipped his head and looked into her eyes. "I believe you do."

$\mathcal{I}$F YOU WANT TO KNOW MORE ABOUT
KATIE AND JOSH, BE SURE TO READ

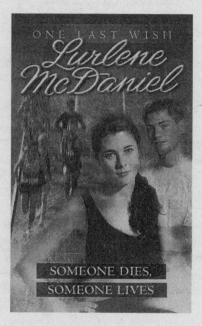

ON SALE NOW FROM BANTAM BOOKS
0-553-29842-9

Excerpt from *Someone Dies, Someone Lives* by Lurlene McDaniel
Copyright © 1992 by Lurlene McDaniel

Published by Bantam Doubleday Dell Books for Young Readers
a division of Random House, Inc.
1540 Broadway, New York, New York 10036

$\mathcal{K}$atie O'Roark feels miserable, though she knows she's incredibly lucky to have received an anonymous gift of money. The money can't buy the new heart she needs or bring back her days as a track star.

A donor is found with a compatible heart, and Katie undergoes transplant surgery. While recuperating, she meets Josh Martel and senses an immediate connection. When Katie decides to start training to realize her dream of running again, Josh helps her meet the difficult challenge.

Will Katie find the strength physically and emotionally to live and become a winner again?

From the corner of her eye, Katie saw a boy with red hair who was about her age. He stood near the doorway, looking nervous. With a start, she realized he was watching her because he kept averting his gaze when she glanced his way. Odd, Katie told herself. Katie had a nagging sense she couldn't place him. As nonchalantly as possible, she rolled her wheelchair closer, picking up a magazine as she passed a table.

She flipped through the magazine, pretending to be interested, all the while glancing discreetly toward the boy. Even though he also picked up a magazine, Katie could tell that he was preoccupied with studying her. Suddenly, she grew self-conscious. Was something wrong with the way she looked? She'd thought she looked better than she had in months when she'd left her hospital room that afternoon. Why was he watching her?

Katie is also featured in the novels *Please Don't Die, She Died Too Young,* and *A Season for Goodbye.*

*I*F YOU WANT TO KNOW MORE ABOUT SARAH,

BE SURE TO READ

ON SALE NOW FROM BANTAM BOOKS
0-553-29811-9

Excerpt from *Mother, Help Me Live* by Lurlene McDaniel
Copyright © 1992 by Lurlene McDaniel

Published by Bantam Doubleday Dell Books for Young Readers
a division of Random House, Inc.
1540 Broadway, New York, New York 10036

*S*arah McGreggor is distraught when she learns she will need a bone marrow transplant to live. And she is shocked to find out that her parents and siblings can't be donors because they aren't her blood relatives. Sarah never knew she was adopted.

As Sarah faces this devastating news, she is granted one last wish by an anonymous benefactor. With hope in her heart, she begins a search for her birth mother, who gave her up fifteen years ago. Sarah's life depends on her finding this woman. But what will Sarah discover about the true meaning of family?

Didn't the letter from JWC say she could spend it on anything she wanted? What could be more important than finding her birth mother? What could be more important than discovering if she had siblings with compatible bone marrow? Her very life could depend on finding these people. Sarah practically jumped up from the sofa. "I've got to go," she said.

*I*F YOU WANT TO KNOW MORE ABOUT ERIC,

BE SURE TO READ

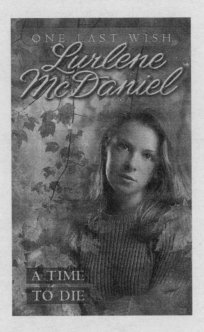

ON SALE NOW FROM BANTAM BOOKS
0-553-29809-7

Excerpt from *A Time to Die* by Lurlene McDaniel
Copyright © 1992 by Lurlene McDaniel

Published by Bantam Doubleday Dell Books for Young Readers
a division of Random House, Inc.
1540 Broadway, New York, New York 10036

S ixteen-year-old Kara Fischer has never considered herself lucky. She doesn't understand why she was born with cystic fibrosis. Despite her daily treatments, each day poses the threat of a lung infection that could put her in the hospital for weeks. But her close friendship with her fellow CF patient Vince and the new feelings she is quickly developing for Eric give her the hope to live one day at a time.

When an anonymous benefactor promises to grant a single wish with no strings attached, Kara finds a way to let the people who have loved and supported her throughout her illness know how much they mean to her. But will there be time for Kara to see her dying wish fulfilled?

"What am I going to do about you, Kara?"

Eric's tone was subdued and so sincere that his question caught her by surprise. "What do you mean?"

"I can't stay away from you."

"You seem to be doing a fine job of it," she said quietly, but without malice.

"I know it seems that way, but you don't know how hard it's been."

She was skeptical. "We just danced together, but after tonight, how will it be between us? Will you still ignore me in the halls? Will you duck into the nearest open door whenever you see me coming?"

He turned his head and she saw his jaw clench. She thought he might walk away, but instead he asked, "What's between you and Vince?"

$\mathcal{J}$F YOU WANT TO KNOW MORE ABOUT MORGAN,
BE SURE TO READ

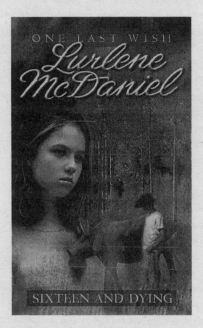

ON SALE NOW FROM BANTAM BOOKS
0-553-29932-8

Excerpt from *Sixteen and Dying* by Lurlene McDaniel
Copyright © 1992 by Lurlene McDaniel

Published by Bantam Doubleday Dell Books for Young Readers
a division of Random House, Inc.
1540 Broadway, New York, New York 10036

*I*t's hard for Anne Wingate and her father to accept the doctors' diagnosis: Anne is HIV-positive. Seven years ago, before blood screening was required, Anne received a transfusion. It saved her life then, but now the harsh reality can't be changed—the blood was tainted. Anne must deal with the inevitable progression of her condition.

When an anonymous benefactor promises to grant Anne a single wish with no strings attached, she decides to spend the summer on a ranch out west. She wants to live as normally as she possibly can. The summer seems even better than she dreamed, especially after she meets Morgan. Anne doesn't confide in Morgan about her condition and doesn't plan to. Then her health begins to deteriorate and she returns home. Is there time for Anne and Morgan to meet again?

Fearfully, Anne stared at her bleeding hand.

Morgan reached beneath her, lifted her, and placed her safely away from the hay and its invisible weapon. "Let me see how bad you're cut."

"It's nothing," Anne said, keeping her hand close to her body. "I'm fine."

"You're not fine. You're bleeding. You may need stitches. Let me wipe it off and examine it."

Her eyes widened, reminding him of a deer trapped in headlights. "No! Don't touch it!"

"But—"

"Please—you don't understand. I—I can't explain. Just don't touch it." Wild-eyed, panicked, she spun, and clutching her hand to her side, she bolted from the barn.

Dumbfounded, Morgan watched her run back toward the cabin.

$\mathcal{Y}$OU MAY ALSO WANT TO READ

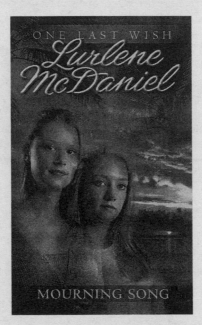

ON SALE NOW FROM BANTAM BOOKS
0-553-29810-0

Excerpt from *Mourning Song* by Lurlene McDaniel
Copyright © 1992 by Lurlene McDaniel

Published by Bantam Doubleday Dell Books for Young Readers
a division of Random House, Inc.
1540 Broadway, New York, New York 10036

*I*t's been months since Dani Vanoy's older sister, Cassie, was diagnosed as having a brain tumor. And now the treatments aren't helping. Dani is furious that she is powerless to help her sister. She can't even convince their mother to take the girls on the trip to Florida Cassie has always longed for.

Then Cassie receives an anonymous letter offering her a single wish. Dani knows she can never make Cassie well, but she is determined to see Cassie's dream come true, with or without their mother's approval.

Dani had rehearsed the speech so many times that even she was beginning to believe it. "It's as if you're supposed to do this. While we don't know who gave you the money for a wish, I think you should use it to get something you've always wanted. Listen, even a trillion dollars can't make you well, but the money you've gotten can help you have some fun. I say let's go for it! You deserve to see the ocean, whether Mom agrees or not. I'm going to help you make your wish come true."

*I*F YOU WANT TO KNOW MORE ABOUT RICHARD
HOLLOWAY AND JENNY CRAWFORD,
BE SURE TO READ

ON SALE NOW FROM BANTAM BOOKS
0-553-56134-0

Excerpt from *The Legacy: Making Wishes Come True* by Lurlene McDaniel
Copyright © 1993 by Lurlene McDaniel

Published by Bantam Doubleday Dell Books for Young Readers
a division of Random House, Inc.
1540 Broadway, New York, New York 10036

*W*ho is JWC, and how was the One Last Wish Foundation created? Follow JWC's struggle for survival against impossible odds and the intertwining stories of love and friendship that developed into a legacy of giving. And discover the power that one individual's determination can have, in this extraordinary novel of hope.

"*I had my physician call the ER doctor and afterward, when we discussed their conversation, he suggested that I get her to a specialist as quickly as possible.*"

"*A specialist at Boston Children's,*" *Richard said with a nod.* "*What kind of specialist?*"

"*A pediatric oncologist.*"

Before Richard could say another word, Jenny's grandmother spoke. "*A cancer specialist,*" *Marian said, her voice catching.* "*They believe Jenny has leukemia.*"

𝒥F YOU WANT TO KNOW MORE ABOUT KATIE,
CHELSEA, AND LACEY,
BE SURE TO READ

ON SALE NOW FROM BANTAM BOOKS
0-553-56262-2

Excerpt from *Please Don't Die* by Lurlene McDaniel
Copyright © 1993 by Lurlene McDaniel

Published by Bantam Doubleday Dell Books for Young Readers
a division of Random House, Inc.
1540 Broadway, New York, New York 10036

*W*hen Katie O'Roark receives an invitation from the One Last Wish Foundation to spend the summer at Jenny House, she eagerly says yes. Katie is ever grateful to JWC, the unknown person who gave her the gift that allowed her to receive a heart transplant. Now Katie is asked to be a "big sister" to others who, like her, face daunting medical problems: Amanda, a thirteen-year-old victim of leukemia; Chelsea, a fourteen-year-old candidate for a heart transplant; and Lacey, a sixteen-year-old diabetic who refuses to deal with her condition. As the summer progresses, the girls form close bonds and enjoy the chance to act "just like healthy kids." But when a crisis jeopardizes one girl's chance of fulfilling her dreams, they discover true friendship and its power to endure beyond this life.

"Me, too. I don't know what I'd do without you, Katie. Whenever I think about last summer, about how you were so close to dying . . ."

She didn't allow him to complete his sentence. "Every day is new, every morning, Josh. I'm glad I got a second chance at life. And after meeting the people here at Jenny House, after making friends with Amanda, Chelsea, and even Lacey, I want all of us to live forever."

He grinned. "Forever's a long time."

She returned his smile. "All right, then at least until we're all old and wrinkled."

ℐf YOU WANT TO KNOW MORE ABOUT
KATIE AND CHELSEA, BE SURE TO READ

ON SALE NOW FROM BANTAM BOOKS
0-553-56263-0

Excerpt from *She Died Too Young* by Lurlene McDaniel
Copyright © 1994 by Lurlene McDaniel

Published by Bantam Doubleday Dell Books for Young Readers
a division of Random House, Inc.
1540 Broadway, New York, New York 10036

*C*helsea James and Katie O'Roark met at Jenny House and spent a wonderful summer together.

Now Chelsea and her mother are staying with Katie as Chelsea awaits news about a heart transplant. While waiting for a compatible donor, Chelsea meets Jillian, a kind, funny girl who's waiting for a heart-lung transplant. The two girls become fast friends. When Chelsea meets Jillian's brother, he awakens feelings in her she's never known before. But as her medical situation grows desperate, Chelsea finds herself in a contest for her life against her best friend. Is it fair that there's a chance for only one of them to survive?

"Don't you see? There's one donor coming in. Only one. Who will the doctors save? Who will get the transplant?"

For a moment Josh stared blankly as her question sank in. "Katie, you don't know for sure there's only one donor."

"Yes, I do. There's only one. One heart. Two lungs. The doctor said the donor's family had given permission for all her organs to be donated." Katie's voice had risen with the tide of panic rising in her. "There's two people in need and only one heart."

Katie and Chelsea are also featured in the novels *Please Don't Die* and *A Season for Goodbye*.

$\mathscr{I}$F YOU WANT TO KNOW MORE ABOUT LACEY,

BE SURE TO READ

ON SALE NOW FROM BANTAM BOOKS
0-553-56264-9

Excerpt from *All the Days of Her Life* by Lurlene McDaniel
Copyright © 1994 by Lurlene McDaniel

Published by Bantam Doubleday Dell Books for Young Readers
a division of Random House, Inc.
1540 Broadway, New York, New York 10036

Out of control—that's how Lacey Duval feels in almost every aspect of her life. There's nothing she can do about her parents' divorce, there's nothing she can do about the death of her young friend, there's nothing she can do about having diabetes—that's what Lacey believes.

After a special summer at Jenny House, Lacey is determined to put her problems behind her. When she returns to high school, she is driven to become a part of the in crowd. But Lacey thinks fitting in means losing weight and hiding her diabetes. She starts skipping meals and experimenting with her medication—sometimes ignoring it altogether.

Her friends from the summer caution her to face her problems before catastrophe strikes. Is it too late to stop the destructive process Lacey has set in motion?

She went hot and cold all over. It was as if he'd shone a light into some secret part of her heart and something dark and ugly had crawled out. She had rejected Jeff because she didn't want a sick boyfriend. She'd said as much to Katie at Jenny House.

"It's any sickness, Jeff. It's mine too. I hate it all. I know it's not your fault, but it's not mine either."

"I'll bet no one at your school knows you're a diabetic."

She said nothing.

"I'm right, aren't I?"

"It's none of your business."

"You know, Lacey, you're the person who won't accept that you have a disease. Why is that?"

She whirled on him. "How can you ask me that when you've just admitted that girls drop you once they discover you're a bleeder? You of all people should understand why I keep my little secret."

Lacey is also featured in the novels *Please Don't Die* and *A Season for Goodbye*.

$\mathcal{I}$F YOU WANT TO KNOW MORE ABOUT KATIE,
CHELSEA, AND LACEY, BE SURE TO READ

ON SALE NOW FROM BANTAM BOOKS
0-553-56265-7

Excerpt from *A Season for Goodbye* by Lurlene McDaniel
Copyright © 1995 by Lurlene McDaniel

Published by Bantam Doubleday Dell Books for Young Readers
a division of Random House, Inc.
1540 Broadway, New York, New York 10036

Together again. It's been a year since Katie O'Roark, Chelsea James, and Lacey Duval shared a special summer at Jenny House. The girls have each spent the year struggling to fit into the world of the healthy. Now they're back, this time as "big sisters" to a new group of girls who also face life-threatening illnesses.

But even as the friends strive to help their "little sisters" face the future together, they must separately confront their own expectations. Katie must decide between an old flame and an exciting scholarship far from home. Chelsea must overcome her fear of romance. And Lacey must convince the boy she loves that her feelings for him can be trusted.

When tragedy strikes Jenny House, each of the girls knows that things can never be the same. Will Lacey, Chelsea, and Katie find a way to carry on the legacy of Jenny House? Can their special friendship endure?

"Over here!" Katie called. "I found it."

Chelsea and Lacey hurried to where Katie was crouched, digging through a pile of dead leaves. The tepee was partially buried, and Chelsea held her breath, hoping that the laminated photo and Jillian's diamond stud earring were still tied to it.

"It's come apart," Katie said, lifting up the twigs in three parts. But from the corner of one of the sticks, the laminated photo dangled, and from its center the diamond caught the afternoon sunlight.

The photo looked faded, but Amanda still smiled from the center of their group. Chelsea felt a lump form in her throat. These days, she and Katie and Lacey looked older, more mature, healthier too. But Amanda looked the same, her gamine smile frozen in time. And ageless.

Katie took the photo from Lacey's trembling fingers. "We were quite a bunch, weren't we?"

$\mathcal{Y}$OU CAN READ MORE ABOUT

MANY OF YOUR FAVORITE CHARACTERS FROM

THE ONE LAST WISH BOOKS IN

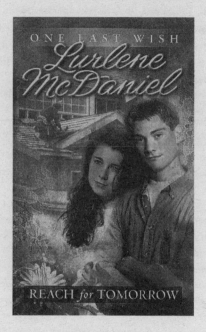

ON SALE NOW FROM BANTAM BOOKS
0-553-57109-5

Excerpt from *Reach for Tomorrow* by Lurlene McDaniel
Copyright © 1999 by Lurlene McDaniel

Published by Bantam Doubleday Dell Books for Young Readers
a division of Random House, Inc.
1540 Broadway, New York, New York 10036

$\mathcal{K}$atie O'Roark is thrilled to learn that Jenny House is being rebuilt. After the fire last year, Katie thought she could never return to the camp, where she spent the summers with young men and women like her who faced medical odds that were stacked against them. But thanks to Richard Holloway's efforts, Katie and her longtime friends Lacey and Chelsea will work as counselors once again. They'll be joined by Megan Charnell, Morgan Lancaster, and Eric Lawrence, who are newcomers to Jenny House but who have experienced the generosity of the One Last Wish Foundation.

It's not until Katie arrives at camp that she discovers that Josh Martel, her former boyfriend, is also a counselor. Katie and Josh broke up a year ago, when Katie decided to go away to college. Being near Josh again brings back a flood of old emotions for Katie. And when Josh confronts unexpected adversity, Katie knows she has to work out her feelings for him. Through the heart transplant she underwent years ago, Katie miraculously received a gift of new life. Now she must discover how to make the most of that precious gift and choose her future.

She stopped. By now tears had filled her eyes and her heart felt as if it might break. She truly believed that God had heard her prayer. What she did not know was whether or not he would grant her request. Against great odds, God had given her a new heart when she'd desperately needed one. And he had brought Josh into her life as well. She believed that with all her heart and soul. Now there was nothing more she could do except wait. And have faith.

Katie lifted her arms in the moonlight in supplication to the heavens.

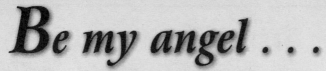

Get *online* with your *favorite author!*

www.lurlenemcdaniel.com

The official *Lurlene McDaniel* Website!

- *interactive author forum*

- *exclusive chapter excerpts*

- *contests and giveaways*

and much more!